D1414421

CREED

TRISHA LEAVER
LINDSAY CURRIE

CREED

flux®
Woodbury, Minnesota

First Edition
First Printing, 2014

Book design by Bob Gaul
Cover design by Lisa Novak
Cover image: iStockphoto.com/22216886/©ghoststone
iStockphoto.com/23954028/©ghoststone
iStockphoto.com/25345652/©ghoststone
iStockphoto.com/22685062/©peter zelei

Flux, an imprint of Llewellyn Worldwide Ltd.

This is a work of fiction. Names, characters, places, and incidents are either the product of the author's imagination or are used fictitiously, and any resemblance to actual persons living or dead, business establishments, events, or locales is entirely coincidental. Cover models used for illustrative purposes only and may not endorse or represent the book's subject.

Library of Congress Cataloging-in-Publication Data
Leaver, Trisha.
  Creed/Trisha Leaver, Lindsay Currie.—First edition.
    pages cm
  Summary: When their car breaks down, Dee, her boyfriend Luke, and his brother Mike walk through a winter storm to take refuge in a nearby deserted town called Purity Springs, but in the morning they see the town is populated with a deadly cult and find themselves at the mercy of the charismatic leader, Elijah Hawkins.
  ISBN 978-0-7387-4080-5
[1. Ghost towns—Fiction. 2. Cults—Fiction. 3. Religious leaders—Fiction. 4. Escapes—Fiction.] I. Currie, Lindsay. II. Title.
PZ7.L428Cr 2014
[Fic]—dc23

2014025039

Flux
Llewellyn Worldwide Ltd.
2143 Wooddale Drive
Woodbury, MN 55125-2989
www.fluxnow.com

Printed in the United States of America

"If you want to go fast, go alone. If you want to go far, go together."—African proverb

Thanks, Bri, for eighteen years of going far together.
—*Trisha*

To my husband and kiddos. I hope I can make you guys even half as proud as you make me.
—*Lindsay*

Three days.
Three of us went in.
Three of us came out.
None of us even a shadow of who we once were.

ONE

The car rolled to a stop on the side of the dirt road. I swore, frustrated that I'd left my jacket at home rather than cover up my new shirt. The rain we'd been driving through had quickly turned to ice, leaving the edges of the country road glossy and slick. It was cold and wet out there. And now I had to walk. Without a coat.

Luke yanked his earbuds out and tossed them onto the dashboard, then slammed the car into park. Not that it was going to go anywhere in drive. It had pretty much sputtered itself to a slow death.

"Where are we?" I asked, stepping out of the car. My feet slid out from under me, and I had to grab onto the mirror to keep myself from falling.

"No idea," Luke said as he tapped the gas gauge to see

if he could get it to move. "Probably somewhere between Watertown and Albany."

"Way to narrow it down," I said, popping the trunk in search of a sweatshirt or jacket. "That's what … a three-hundred-plus mile range you've rattled off?

I turned to Luke's brother, Mike, hoping he'd been paying better attention. "Where are we?"

Mike shrugged. "No clue, Dee. Sorry."

I sighed. Not that I'd been watching the signs either. I'd spent the last hour with my head buried in my Spanish book, more worried about Monday's test than directions.

I rifled through my bag in the trunk, looking for something warm to throw over my shirt, but it wasn't like I'd packed for hiking. All I had was a pair of heeled boots, some jeans, a silky thing that couldn't even pass for pajamas, and no one to blame but myself. It'd been over four years since I'd had to worry about having a *just-in-case* bag packed, and I'd gotten lazy. Or maybe too comfortable. Now I was looking at a case of frostbite as punishment.

I reached for Luke's duffel bag and pulled out a pair of boxer shorts, a toothbrush, and a string of condoms. "Seriously? That's what you packed?" I giggled as I shoved the condoms back into the bag, praying Mike hadn't seen them. Luke's choice of items was perfectly fine with me.

Luke smiled, his grin more devious than sorry. "It's not like you gave me any idea where we were going or what you had planned. What else was I supposed to think?"

Nothing. He'd pretty much nailed it.

"Mind if I borrow this?" I asked as I pulled on one of

Luke's practice shirts. I gave it a quick sniff and decided the brown patches were actually dirt from the football field. Old dirt at that. It was warm, the fabric soft as if it had been recently washed, and it smelled 100 percent like him.

I snuggled deeper into the fabric. Something about this small part of him surrounding me made me feel safer and less on edge. "What time did we leave?"

"Two, maybe two thirty," Mike responded. "Why?"

"No reason," I said as I climbed back into the car and dug myself into Luke's shoulder. It was a little past five, which meant we'd been on the road for about three hours. The concert was at seven in Albany, so I assumed we were about halfway there. But we'd stopped twice. Once because Mike had to pee, the second time because my stomach was growling louder than the engine. I figured about five minutes for the first stop, more for the second—the whole Twinkie vs. Ding Dong debate at the gas station and all— so that would put us about...

Who was I kidding? I had no clue where we were.

Leaning over Luke, I jammed the keys back into the ignition. I barely had enough time to get a look at the gas gauge before it died again, leaving us in frozen silence.

"How is it that we stopped at a convenience store two hours ago, ended up with a pound of Twinkies, and not a single one of us thought to get gas?"

Luke's mouth turned upward into one of those sexy, lopsided grins that usually got him off the hook. "Don't look at me. I'm map-guy, remember? Once we pulled off the highway, I had to focus on the directions. Gas . . . supplies . . . Twinkies, that was all you and Mike."

He fumbled around on the floor of the car and pulled up the crinkled map. I-90 was jammed with traffic, so we'd pulled off about an hour ago, hoping to make better time. Unfortunately for me, map-guy and gas-guy couldn't co-exist.

"You know how you asked me why colleges don't allow hot plates in the dorm rooms?" Mike teased.

"Yeah, why?" Luke replied.

"Well, you're the reason."

I fought off a grin as I watched Luke think, his fingers tapping against his leg. Luke was brilliant, could solve an advanced calculus problem with very little effort. He had every play for the last three football games stored in his head and had scored a full academic ride to college. It was the simpler things like gas gauges and programing the DVR that threw him off. It was one of the thousands of details I loved about Luke. Somehow, it was both cute and irritating at the same time.

"If you're saying that an unattended hot plate is a greater fire risk than, say, an iron or a candle, then you're wrong. I gotta think that, statistically speaking—"

"Let it go," I said, cutting Luke off. If we were betting on odds, then statistically speaking it'd be Mike and his bong that burned down the dorm.

Luke turned to me, his eyes softening as he took in my shivering state. "Sorry, Dee. I was listening to music and zoned out. I didn't even think about gas."

"It's not your fault," I groaned.

It wasn't his fault; it was mine. You'd think after four years of living with the Hoopers, I would've learned to keep the gas tank full. They were old, old enough to be my grandparents, which meant each time their Buick left the driveway for the two-mile trek to bingo it came back with a full tank of gas. No exceptions. Mr. Hooper would scold me seven ways to Sunday if he knew we'd run out of gas, then he'd take Luke's car to the station himself and fill it up. I'd be embarrassed and Luke would feign guilt, but neither of us would've complained.

The Hoopers had taken me in, a ward of the state with no home and no real family to speak of, and made me feel like one of their own. They didn't need to, and God knows the miserable four hundred and fifty dollars a month the state paid them didn't begin to cover my expenses, but they still let me stay. For that, I'd sit there quietly and let them rant about how irresponsible it was for us to get stuck on the side of the road because of something so stupid.

Mike leaned into the front seat and scanned the horizon. "It's no biggie. We'll call a tow truck."

I fished my cell phone out of my pocket and stared at the screen. No signal. I don't know what I was expecting; there hadn't been a signal since we'd pulled off the highway.

It was getting dark, there wasn't a person in sight, and we had no clue where we were. Great, now all we needed was a skinny, pale girl in a bikini, a big guy in a mask sporting a chain saw, and a sheriff turned zombie and we had the makings for a perfect horror movie.

"No signal," I said, holding up my phone for Mike to see. "Try yours."

"Nothing," they both said in unison.

Wiping the thin layer of fog from the window, I looked out into the vanishing daylight. Except for the three-foot-high stalks of dying crops shaking gently in the wind, I saw nothing. Heard nothing.

"We're in the middle of Nowhere, New York, with a good fifty-mile walk to the last gas station we passed," I said, inching closer to Luke. "We need a plan, or we're going to miss..."

I trailed off, not wanting to ruin Luke's surprise. He had no clue where we were going. No idea I'd been scraping money together for the better part of five months to get him those concert tickets.

"Miss what?" Luke asked, pulling me closer. He dropped a line of kisses on my neck, his breath heavy and sweet in my ear. He was taunting me, trying to get me to spill my secret.

"Nothing, but we need to get back on the road," I said, unwinding myself from his grip.

Luke eased back, dropping that happy-go-lucky attitude of his. It'd taken him a long time to get to this point with me, to recognize the fear in my voice and understand that I wasn't the defiant, hardened foster kid everybody assumed I was.

"Relax, Dee. It's gonna be fine." Luke pulled his jersey around me tighter, his gaze lingering on the number three—his number—on my chest, and a look of appreciation lit up his face. "Looks better on you than me."

It actually looked best rolled up in a ball at the foot of

his bed next to my shoes and jeans, but I didn't say that. Not with Mike listening from the back seat.

"Stay here," Luke said as he slipped on his gloves. "There's got to be a town nearby. Mike and I will go find some gas."

I stared at him, my mind racing through a thousand juvenile scenarios. Each of them ended up with me hacked to pieces by the local crazy man. "Yeah ... no. I'm going with you."

I cocked my head, daring Luke to challenge me. He smiled, shrugged out of his jacket, and wrapped it around my shoulders. His fingers wound tightly into mine and I sighed, feeling a momentary sense of peace. Luke would walk through hell for me, and, given the walls I'd made him tear down when we first started dating, I had no reason to doubt him now.

The hazy possibility of a town shone through the sleet, the lights barely visible from where we sat. Even if Luke was right and we were close to another gas station, I doubted we'd make it there before we froze to death.

I forced myself to open my door again, the wind cutting through me like a steel blade. Luke was already rummaging through a black bag in the trunk. He found a flashlight and flicked it on, the narrow beam illuminating the side of the road.

"Let's go," he said. "The sooner we find gas, the sooner we can get back on the road."

I looked at Luke, my gaze landing on what appeared to be a tire iron lodged in his left hand. "You bringing that?" I asked, suddenly wishing we'd decided to sit in the car, blow off the concert, and flag down the next person who drove by.

"Sure am," Luke said.

I shook my head and fought the urge to laugh. There was zero chance of someone helping us now. I mean, who in their right mind was going to stop for three kids, especially one carrying a tire iron?

I glanced back toward the car, unnerved to see that it was quickly fading away behind us. We'd barely walked a quarter-mile, and yet our car was already veiled in ice. I put my hand in Luke's, praying that the town was closer than it looked.

TWO

The town definitely wasn't as close as it looked. My feet hurt and my fingers were numb by the time we hit the outskirts. I probably would've sat down right there on the side of the road in a pile of muddy slush had it not been for the annoying siren echoing through the silence.

"What is that?" I asked, my head pounding in time with the two-beat wail.

"Sirens," Mike replied.

"Yeah, thanks, I got that," I muttered, then turned to Luke. "I meant, why are they going off?"

Luke shrugged and scanned the area, same as me, in search of a mushroom cloud, a tornado, a wall of water . . . anything that would explain why the emergency sirens had been set off. Except for a bank of gray clouds hovering in the distance, the horizon was clear. No sign of a deadly storm, a world-ending apocalypse, or a zombie attack. Absolutely nothing.

Not only that, but as far as I could tell, there was nobody around to warn. What looked like cars were up ahead, but they were stationary—no blaring horns or mufflers. Had it not been for the two expensive-looking tractors and a set of fresh tire tracks lining the road, I would've assumed the town was abandoned.

"Don't worry," Luke said, squeezing my hand tighter. "We'll hit the first gas station we see, grab some gas, and get back on the road." He leaned in and ran his hand across the back of my neck, drawing me closer. "Maybe you want to tell me what the big surprise is now? I may find that gas a little faster if I had something to look forward to and all."

"Not gonna happen," I said and pushed him away. He turned to Mike, no doubt planning to bait his younger brother for information. I held my hand up, warning Mike to keep his mouth shut. "Don't you even think about it!"

Mike slapped Luke on the shoulder, bracing himself for the punch that would undoubtedly follow. "Sorry, but the boss says no."

Luke's chuckle felt forced, like he was trying to keep the conversation light despite the fact that the sirens were getting louder by the minute. "Yeah? And when did you start taking your orders from her?"

Mike grinned, that stupid, mischievous twinkle marring his eyes. "I don't, but we both know *you* do. Walls are thin back home. Really thin."

"Shut up!" I shouted, picking up my pace. There were

some things I'd rather not think about, and Mike listening to me and Luke … yeah, that was one of them.

The first shadow of a building appeared, the sleet making its brick exterior shine with a coldness that crept into my soul. I stopped at the base of the steps and stared up at the words engraved above the door: *Purity Springs Savings and Trust*. Next to the bank was a grocery store and across the street was a dry cleaner, a small café, and what appeared to be a string of white-clapboard community buildings connected to a chapel.

I stopped in the middle of the street and tugged Luke to a halt beside me. Other than the sirens blaring in my ears, it was still. Dead. No howling dogs, no crying children, no cars speeding away from impending danger.

I shuddered. The vacant street, the splatter of slush against concrete, the ancient-looking buildings all hovered around us. It was seriously creepy, and I fumbled in my purse for the tiny canister of mace I always carried. Not that there was anybody to spray. The place was a ghost town.

"Where is everybody?" I wondered out loud.

"No clue," Luke yelled, competing with the sirens. "Not sure I care, either," he added, pointing down the street.

I had to squint in order to make out the faint sign about a quarter-mile up. It wasn't the words, but rather the familiar-shaped rectangles jutting up from the ground that gave it away. "Gas station," I squealed and took off running.

The sun was about to set, the orange glow painting the streets in a dim light. For as deathly silent as this place was, I could've sworn I saw shadows. They were nothing more than flashes of black darting behind the buildings, but they were there. My rational mind knew it was probably just the last bit of sunlight changing positions. But logical thinking was no match for my imagination, and I found myself squeezing the small canister of mace, my hand sweating as I melded it with my palm.

Mr. Hooper had given it to me the week I came to live with them. I was barely thirteen and trusted nobody, including myself. I hadn't seen my parents for over a year at that point. The state had finally taken me away from them permanently when my father's interest in me went from a simple punching bag to something else. I'd been bounced between three different foster homes and kicked out of two residential programs when the Hoopers finally agreed to give me "one last shot." That last shot came with a lot of rules and weekly, court-mandated counseling, but eventually the Hoopers wore me down and got me talking when all I wanted to do was hide.

Mr. Hooper tucked the mace into my hand the day I started school, told me the first step to getting beyond my past was to take control of my present. I took it because having that small weapon made me feel less like a victim and more like a girl you didn't want to mess with. Now the mace came with me everywhere.

Turning back, I scanned the street for Mike. He may have been the third wheel on this trip, but he was Luke's brother, and at the end of the day, he was always good for a few laughs. That and he had our concert tickets in his wallet.

"You see Mike anywhere?" I asked.

Luke circled his hand in the direction of everything and

nothing. "Yeah, he's fine. He's checking the place out, same as us."

I sighed and searched the empty street once more. We had to stay together; it was stupid to be splitting up like this.

"Relax, Dee. There's no on here," Luke said. "They probably evacuated when the sirens went off. I'm sure it's nothing more than a false alarm."

I shrugged and kept going, wanting to get out of this place as soon as possible. This town, with its eerie silence and deserted streets, made me feel weak, like I was being watched...cornered. And I hated that feeling.

Sensing my unease, Luke tugged me to a stop and forced me to look at him. "I'm not gonna let anything happen to you."

I smiled and tried to look reassured. I believed him, or at least most of me did. The rest was hanging onto seventeen years' worth of crap.

He ran the pad of his thumb over my cheek, the familiar look of determination flickering in his eyes. "Dee, you believe me, right?"

"Yeah, but Mike..." I trailed off. My throat was already getting sore. If I wasn't careful, competing with the sirens would eventually make me both deaf *and* mute.

The darkened street stretched ahead of us and I exhaled, taking comfort in the sight of Mike's figure in the window of the brightly lit gas station. The parking lot was full, several cars sitting side-by-side. Empty. Luke tapped on the open door of a standard-issue blue Ford, his mind no doubt traveling the same unsettling path as mine. He and I had lived in the same town for almost four years now, and we knew full-well that when there was an emergency, not everyone listened. There were always a few idiots who stayed behind, believing they were stronger and smarter and capable of out-smarting Mother Nature. Not here. Apparently, everybody is this town was a law-abiding citizen.

Luke placed his hand on my shoulder. He was probably just trying to get my attention, but it scared the crap out of me. I screamed out a four-lettered reaction and jerked away.

"Down, girl," Luke said with a smirk.

He motioned toward the gas station's windows, where Mike was waving us in. I laughed nervously as the bell above the doorway jingled, signaling our entrance. I half expected a grease-covered kid to come and see what we wanted. Instead, I was met by nothing but empty aisles.

"Oh thank God," I moaned, uncovering my ears as the door swung shut, dampening the high-pitched wail of the sirens.

"No phone, but I found a gas can," Mike said as he proudly waved the shiny red container in the air. "It's empty though."

"No problem. We'll fill it up," Luke said. "I'll leave a twenty on the counter to cover it."

"It's not that easy," Mike muttered, banging on the tiny silver bell perched on the counter. Nobody answered his call, but he continued hammering away at the bell anyway. "Sure, there's gas, but we can't get to it without someone working here."

Luke peered down the hall. "Hello? Ah, we need some

gas. Anyone here?" Turning back, he shrugged and did another quick sweep of the counter. "No phone. No keys to the cars parked in the lot. No gas attendant. This place is completely empty. I say we take what we need and go."

Mike lifted the empty can and shoved it in Luke's face. "That's the problem. There's no way to take what we need. The pumps won't work without someone here to turn them on."

"Bullshit," Luke said as he fished out his wallet and handed Mike his ATM card. "This place has automated pumps. Run my card through."

"Already tried," Mike said. "I swiped my card five times and nothing happened."

I'd always assumed that when you swiped a card in one of those machines, it...well...it simply went through. Apparently not. Even in crappy little Podunk towns, people were still necessary.

"You used to work at a Seven Eleven," Mike said, motioning me forward. "Come figure this out."

"I think someone needs to authorize the card," I said as I stepped behind the counter. "And I only worked there for two days. They hadn't taught me how to run the pumps yet."

I knew some of the buttons on the cash register from my brief stint last summer at the mini-mart. I'd clocked less than sixteen hours there before I realized it was a waste of time and left in search of something less boring. I was still looking.

"There's a button or a key code or something. I'm pretty sure it has something to do with the cash register, but I'm not positive," I said.

Luke stepped to my side, his fingers whispering across the buttons of the register. "Do you recognize any of these?"

I did. Problem was, without the four-digit security code, no one was accessing those pumps. I pressed the enter key to be sure, hoping that whoever owned this place had left in a hurry and neglected to secure the pumps. I got a blue screen and a flashing curser, confirming what I already knew. "You need a code to unlock the pumps."

I felt the warmth of Luke's arm around me, knew he was trying hard to be patient in a horrible situation. "Try one-two-three-four," he suggested.

I pushed virtually every button, groaning loudly when I got nothing in return but a chorus of alarms sounding from the machine.

"Forget it," Mike said as he moved toward the door. "Screw the machines; I'll get us some gas."

"Wait up." Luke jogged over to his brother. I followed them to the doorway, wondering whether Mike planned on kicking the crap out of the pumps or sucking the gas out of the parked cars. Neither seemed promising.

Luke laid a palm on the glass, gave a quick shove, and pushed the door open a few inches. A blast of frigid air swept in, swirling a few crumpled pieces of paper out of the trash can and onto the floor. "Stay in here, Dee. Maybe get us some snacks for the road," he said. "It's freezing out, and from the looks of those clouds, the ice is going to turn to snow."

"Yeah, no problem," I said as I surveyed the mini-mart, taking special note of the chips aisle. "The least this town can do is feed us for our trouble."

I ducked back behind the counter and grabbed a paper bag from underneath. A couple of turns down the aisles and I had it filled with favorites—a Diet Coke for me, more Twinkies for Mike, and a soda and some pretzels for Luke. I eyed the box of beef jerky on the counter, my mind wandering back home. There'd been a big hunk of meat defrosting in the refrigerator when I left. The crock-pot was already simmering, and Mrs. Hooper had a five-pound bag of apples ready to be cored. Apple pie. She was making an apple pie for dessert, and damn if I wasn't a tad bit sorry for leaving now.

A stick of beef jerky couldn't come close to satisfying my drooling imagination, so I tossed it back onto the rack and snagged an entire bag of M&Ms instead. I opened my wallet and did a quick tally before tossing down a five and scribbling out an IOU for the remaining ten. Once we got out of here, I'd mail them a check for the difference because I was *never* coming back here again.

The door whipped open and I dropped my bag, nearly lost it for a second before I realized it was only Luke. The look on his face was all the answer I needed, but I asked anyway. "You get the pumps working?"

"Nope."

I craned my neck to see around him, expecting Mike to follow him in. Luke caught my gaze and laughed, kind of a half-snort that let me know whatever Mike was doing, he found it amusing. "He's around the corner puking his guts out. I told him it was idiotic, but the dumbass insisted on sucking the gas out of a car anyway."

I shook my head, gagging at the thought. The image of

Mike vomiting up gasoline was too much for even my iron stomach. "That's nasty. Why did you let him do that?"

Luke chuckled. "You know Mike."

I did. I'd been watching Luke back Mike's big mouth out of fights for the better part of two years. It had become a weekly Friday night activity.

"Don't worry. The odds of him having swallowed enough to do any real harm are slim to none. The first taste had him heaving."

"But what are we supposed to do now? It's gonna be dark soon, and there's no gas."

"What do you want to do?" Luke asked, his tone slowly going from playful to serious. That had me worried.

"Why don't we take a car? There have got to be at least a dozen sitting out there," I suggested.

Luke nodded, his eyes scanning the road outside. "There are, but there aren't any keys. I checked every car in the lot while Mike was working on the gas situation."

"So?" I said, not seeing the problem. If anybody knew how to hotwire a car, it was Luke. He was insanely smart. He could probably tell you the chemical composition of each wire in that engine, never mind how to connect them to create a spark.

Luke laughed. "In theory, I suppose I could tell you how to splice the two ignition wires to generate an electrical spark that would ignite the air-fuel combustion necessary to get the engine started. But to do it in real life…yeah, no. Sorry, Dee, but I have no clue how to hotwire a car."

I went to say something, but he cut me off with a wave of

his hand. "And before you ask, Mike doesn't either. If he did, he wouldn't be puking right now."

"So what, we stay here and wait until somebody comes back?"

"No, I say we head farther into town and see if we can find somebody home. Somebody with a phone."

"Okay. I mean, it's a tiny town, and people in small towns are nice, right?"

"Yep," Luke said, a smile spreading across his face. "No matter what happens tonight, thank you. I have no idea what you planned for me, but I know it's going to be amazing." Dropping a kiss on my forehead, he banged on the window of the station, signaling Mike to hurry up. "Ready?"

"Yup," I said, gathering up the contents of my spilled bag. I was having some serious doubts about wandering around this town at night, but we didn't have much of a choice. The weather was getting worse and it'd be dark soon. At least here, inside the gas station, it was warm, full of my favorite foods, and a lot quieter than outside. Plus, there were plenty of places to hide. Counters to wedge myself under. Aisles to duck behind. Bathrooms with locks. If there was anything I could take away from my childhood, it was that finding ways to make yourself invisible didn't make you a chicken, it made you smart.

"Maybe we should stay here and see if somebody comes back," I said.

Luke saw the fear in my eyes and reached out for my hand. "I'll tell you what, Dee. Give us a half-hour to take a look around. If we don't find a house or another gas station, we'll head back here."

I nodded, fearing that if I spoke, my voice would crack and give away how scared I truly was. I had no idea what we were going to find, not a clue where these deserted side streets would take us, but it didn't matter. It wasn't like there was anybody useful, or harmful, around here to bother us.

THREE

It started to snow the minute we turned the corner off the main street. The flakes were so big you could follow their twisted path to the ground, catching a glimpse of the lacy pattern before they melted into the pavement. I concentrated on each individual flake, carefully stepping around their fleeting outlines as we made our way out of town.

"You cold?" Luke asked.

I was beyond cold and it hurt to breathe, each breath burning its way through my lungs. "You think maybe we would've been better off heading back to the car?" I asked.

"Nope." Luke took off his baseball hat and put it on my head. "No gas. No heat. Besides, there are some houses up ahead. There's got to be somebody home." He tucked the tire iron under his arm and took both of my freezing hands in his, massaging them, and I sighed as that little bit of warmth he offered transferred to me.

Following his eyes, I focused in on the faint lights up ahead. The orange glow had a distinct pattern—linear and perfectly spaced. "Streetlights," I said, thoughts of a warm house and a phone guiding my steps. "There has to be somebody home up there."

"For sure. I can't imagine *everybody* left when the sirens went off. That would be too orderly." Mike paused briefly, the intensity in his voice fading away as he heaved into a nearby bush. "Holy crap, that gas is going to kill me."

"How much did you swallow?" Luke asked, jumping back when another stream of vomit hit the ground near his feet. "That stuff will tear your insides up."

I heard the concern in Luke's voice. The way he watched his brother, his hands hovering over Mike's shoulders in case he fell, was sweet. Even on their worst days, Luke still looked out for his younger brother. That protective instinct was in his blood.

Mike spit one last time and straightened up, swiping the sleeve of his sweatshirt across his mouth before he said, "Not much. Besides, I think the last of it is now covering your shoes."

Luke looked down, groaning as he tried to use the snow-covered ground to clean his shoes. All it did was paste blades of dead grass to his already nasty sneakers.

"I'm gonna try my phone one more time." I dug my phone out of my pocket and pressed the home button with my numb finger. There was still no signal, and the idea of knocking on some random stranger's door seemed more appealing each freezing minute.

"I don't understand how there's no signal in this entire town. I mean, don't they have cell phones around here?" I asked.

Luke rubbed my shoulder, no doubt a silent apology for our lousy luck. Less than an hour ago, I'd been on my way to what was probably going to be the best night of my life. The best night of *our* lives. Our two-year anniversary. I glanced at him, amazed he hadn't given up on me long ago.

The plan had been for us to see his favorite band, then head to the hotel. One room for Mike, and a different room for Luke and me. I'd worked on it for months, even had to lie to both Luke's parents and the Hoopers to get everything to come together.

Lying to Luke's mom had been one thing, but lying to Mrs. Hooper was a whole other beast. It was like lying to your grandmother—your sweet old grandmother who made you cookies after school and baked pies at Christmas. Except Mrs. Hooper wasn't my grandmother. She didn't owe me anything. And that made it worse. She didn't have to bake me cookies, take me in, wash my sheets, or go to my parent-teacher conferences, but she did anyway. And I'd gone and lied to her.

Now our seats would be empty and our hotel room...I didn't even want to think about wasting that. Great way to start the weekend: cold, broke, and feeling extremely guilty.

I wiggled another frozen toe and grumbled under my breath as the wind lashed at my cheeks. We were getting dangerously close to the time opening acts were scheduled to go on stage. It wouldn't be long before I had to give up and tell Luke about the super-fantastic night we *weren't* going to have.

I stopped, and Mike nearly slammed into my back. We'd come to an intersection; a three-way stop. I swiveled my head, quickly glancing down each street. They were nearly identical, each yard perfectly maintained and insanely clean—no stray candy wrappers or cans blowing against the curb. Even the streetlights were lit, not a single one flickering.

Luke tilted his head, squinting his eyes to keep out the snow that was falling heavy on his lashes. "You guys hear anything?"

"No," I said. The only sound I heard was the wind tearing through the trees. "Wait! The sirens! They've stopped."

"Yup, so I guess this ringing in my ears is all me," Luke said as he shoved a finger in his ear.

Now that the sirens had stopped, I expected people to start emerging from their houses, their basements, from whatever makeshift storm shelters they'd built in their yards. Mike and Luke were looking around too, each of them mumbling something under their breath.

This place was quiet. Too quiet.

That bank of clouds hovering in the distance was now here, bringing with it a squall that had me shivering. "Doesn't look like anybody's around," I said, taking a step toward the street on the left, searching for the slightest of movements. "Which one do you want to try first?"

"Makes no difference," Mike said, his head swinging from one house to the next. "They've all gotta have phones, right?"

I gestured to a dimly lit house on our right and said, "Sounds good to me. Let's try that one."

"Hang on a sec," Luke said, putting up his hand to stop us. "Let's try there first."

I followed his gaze, my body cringing at the thought of having to snake my way through the dozens of crosses littering the ground. "Ah...that's a cemetery, Luke."

"I know," he said, pausing long enough to point out a structure in the distance. "And that's a utility shed. Ten bucks says they have a can of gas in there for mowers and diggers and stuff."

"Diggers and stuff?" Mike smirked. "Wow, how very technical of you."

I stifled a grin as Luke's eyes narrowed into tiny slits. "Shut up, Mike. I never said I was a construction expert. But hey, since I'm the one with a free ride to college and you're the one failing English, perhaps the construction industry is something you should seriously consider."

"What's that supposed to mean? Are you saying I'm stu—"

Luke cut him off with a rumble of laughter. "I'm not saying anything, Mike. But before we go door-to-door like the Latter-day Saints, maybe we should at least check the shed."

I laughed along with Luke. How did we go from concern over ingesting too much gas to who was smarter in less than five minutes? I took a step forward, determined to force my feet through the gate of the cemetery. I didn't want to go. I would've rather gone the zealot route and knocked on doors. But we lacked the prerequisite religious tracts and black suit coats, so I doubted anybody would take us for much more than a bunch of grungy kids.

I gave the wrought-iron gate a tug, the bottom dragging along the ground as I pulled it open. We weren't far from the shed, maybe a half-dozen crosses or so. One huge breath and a mad dash, and I'd be there.

"These are weird markers," Luke said, sidestepping around an old wooden cross. "No names, not even a date. Who uses wooden markers anyway? I mean, won't they rot?"

Yeah, like the bodies below them, I thought to myself.

Mike crouched down and brushed his hand across the nearest one, dislodging a chunk of the wood. He wiped the dirty slush across the leg of his jeans, then stood up. "Yup, they rot."

With the slush cleared, the cross was easier to see. It was nothing more than two cut pieces of wood laced together with some sort of twine.

"What kind of graveyard do you think this is?" I asked, thinking of the cemetery where the Hoopers' infant son was buried some forty years ago. The Hoopers went there twice a year, on the day their son was born and the day he died, I presumed. I never asked, just went with them and sat in the car, watching and wondering.

I tried not to dwell on it, to think too hard about how ass-backward things seemed. Why God gave kids to monsters like my dad while leaving the Hoopers childless. I guess life messed with you that way sometimes.

The graveyard where the Hoopers' child was buried had granite headstones with intricate carvings, names, and dates, and benches and permanent flower holders. Here they had nothing but some rotted wood held together by moldy string.

"Maybe it's a military cemetery," Mike offered up. "There are dozens of these markers and they're identical, so what else could it be?"

I surveyed the crosses. Half of them were crumbling and everything smelled like wet dirt. "It doesn't matter," I said. I was freezing, and this place was creeping me out. "Let's go and check the shed."

I made it just three steps before Luke slowed to a crawl beside me. "Check that out," he said, motioning to something clear across the yard.

"What is it?" I asked. Trying to make out the faint glow was useless. I put my hand in Luke's and pulled him along with me as I inched closer.

The tiny orange flame danced behind the branches of a willow tree, the tree's slender limbs whipping toward us as the wind gave them life. Beneath it was the dim flicker.

"Is that a candle?" Mike asked.

"I think so," I said, wondering how it was staying lit in this weather. I moved toward the light, my feet sinking deeply into what looked like a freshly dug grave.

"Watch it!" Luke yelled. He grabbed my elbow and yanked me back. "That's bad luck. Really bad. Walk *around* the graves."

I laughed nervously and pulled my shoe out of the muck that was attempting to swallow it. Luke didn't buy into traditional superstitions like black cats, broken mirrors, and ladders, but the few things he did believe, he stuck to hard-core. Given the fact that my feet were sunk ankle-deep in a freakishly primitive graveyard where they probably didn't even use coffins, I figured it couldn't hurt to follow his lead and be overly cautious.

"Can we forget the candle and stick to the shed?" I asked as I pried my other foot free.

Luke tucked his hand deeper into mine and we edged away from the grave, refocusing on the shed. His fingers were cold, frozen into slender ice cubes, but comforting nonetheless. He winked at me out of the corner of my eye and I couldn't help but grin. If I had to be stuck out here in this hell, I was lucky to be here with him.

The shed was old, its sides worn from the weather and its roof sinking in the middle. I groaned as we stepped up to the door. My mood was already black, and the padlock staring back at me was making it worse.

"Locked," Luke said as he turned to face me, a hint of resignation in his voice. His eyes flickered with frustration, and I shrugged.

I was fully prepared to turn around and forget about the shed and its promise of gas when the first crack of metal rang through the night air. It was deafening and I screamed, my entire body convulsing in fear.

Luke pried my hands from my ears, his mouth turning up in a grin. "You honestly thought he'd give up that easily?" he asked, gesturing toward Mike. "The guy that drank gasoline? C'mon, Dee."

The dim moonlight glinted off of the object clenched in Mike's hand. I looked closer, recognizing the tire iron we'd brought with us from the car. Up until then, I'd forgotten we had it.

"Another couple good hits and I think this will break," Mike said as he swung at the padlock again. The sound echoed like a million pieces of broken glass, the contact sending sparks of metal flying.

"Uh, Mike? Do you think that's a good idea?" I asked as I swung my head around, scanning the area for people. The last thing I wanted was to get busted for some kind of sick vandalism. Not to mention that Luke was heading for college in the fall. Desecration of a grave wasn't exactly an appealing thing for schools to see on his record.

Plus, I only had six months until I was legally free and could no longer be considered a ward of the state. Add a crime like vandalizing the dead to my already sketchy past, and I was sure social services would find a way to hang onto me a bit longer.

"Best idea I've had all day," Mike replied. "Especially since it was your boyfriend who made the *let's-get-off-the-highway-and-take-the-creepy-backwoods-road* call." He chuckled as Luke flipped him off.

Actually, it'd been my call. I didn't want to be late for the concert, so Luke had done what he always did…he tried to fix the problem and make me happy by finding an alternate route.

Mike stepped back, widened his stance, and swung the tire iron again. The lock broke, the vibration of the metals colliding traveling through the ground.

"Yes!" Mike shouted, dropping the tire iron. He tossed

the broken lock aside, a muted thunk coming from somewhere in a nearby shrub.

Luke stepped in first, sputtering and brushing cobwebs from his face. "I can't see a damn thing," he said, his arms outstretched in the darkness.

"Here." Mike tossed him the flashlight we'd taken with us from the car. "Use this."

A small beam of light illuminated the dark room. "Gas can, gas can...there's gotta be something useful in here," Luke muttered to himself.

I flipped open my cell phone and used the light from my home screen to navigate the edges of the room. Hooks lined the walls, most of them supporting yard tools. Hedge trimmers, weed whacker, leaf blower. Pickaxe. "Pickaxe? What would somebody need a pickaxe for?" I asked.

"I don't know. Maybe they use it in the winter when people die and the ground is frozen," Luke offered.

I turned to glare at him, not even remotely thankful for his insight. Mike ignored us and continued rifling through some large plastic bins lining the wall, cursing as a large cardboard box toppled over onto his feet.

Papers spilled out and Luke bent down, casting the beam of light across the mess. Dozens of names handwritten in pencil lined the sheets. Next to each name was a date. I reached down and picked up the first sheet I touched. It was a newer one, dated November 5th...two days ago.

"James McDonald, age six. Margaret Elizabeth Cunningham, age fifty-four. Sadie Calbert, age twenty-two," Luke read aloud. He inhaled sharply and began stuffing the papers back into the box. "These are...I think these are death records."

"I can beat that," Mike chimed in. "Check this out."

Luke turned his light in Mike's direction, slowly scanning it upward until a sign came into view: *Purity Springs. Population 152*. He moved the sign aside; another one, nearly identical, was behind it. "'Purity Springs. Population 151,'" Luke read before shuffling yet another sign aside.

"And looky here," Mike said. "This one looks pretty new, not a scratch on it. Says 'Population 149.' That's messed up."

Luke shook his head, grumbling something incoherent under his breath. I stepped aside, forcing myself to focus on the search for gas as opposed to the archaic death records scattered across the floor.

My mind flashed back to the grave we'd passed on the way here. It was new, and I couldn't help but think there was a sign hanging on the side of the road somewhere that read *Purity Springs. Population 148.*

"Finally," Luke called out from somewhere behind me. I couldn't see his body, but I could hear the sound of his knuckles rapping against the thick plastic of what I prayed was a gas can.

I used the light from my phone to scan the shed and found Luke in the back corner. He shook the can, its contents barely sloshing around.

"Crap," he ground out.

"What?" I asked. "It's gas, right?"

"Oh yeah, it's gas." Luke sighed as he unscrewed the cap and took a whiff to be sure. "But from the weight, my guess is it's almost empty. Doubt we'd have enough to get that leaf blower over there started, never mind a car."

Mike took the canister from Luke's hands and gave it one hard shake. "You're right, it's empty," he said, then dropped the canister to his feet. "Town with no people. Gas station with no phone. Now a maintenance shed with no gas. What kind of messed-up place is this?"

The kind that scares the crap out of me, I thought to myself as I sank to my knees and prayed they were both wrong, that there was enough gas not only to start the car, but to get us far away from Purity Springs.

FOUR

We hurried back through the cemetery, weaving around the graves and keeping our voices to a whisper. Between the death records, the messed-up population signs, and the ghost candle, none of us wanted to stick around there any longer than necessary.

The edge of the neighborhood we'd passed through earlier came in to view and I exhaled a breath of relief, excited at the prospect of getting help. I wanted to get back on the road. At this point, I didn't care if we headed to the concert or back to Mrs. Hooper's pot roast. I'd be grateful either way.

"Which street? Which house?" Mike asked. The streetlights cast enough light for me to catch the flicker of indecision in his eyes. I knew what he was thinking: it didn't matter. It was a total crapshoot either way.

I stared down the street in front of me. Black mailboxes

lined the side of the road, and perfectly straight brick walkways led to the front doors. Also black. I counted twelve houses on that street, then turned in a half-circle and counted twelve more on the street to my right. I didn't bother to check the last one; my guess was there were twelve, eerily identical houses lining that street as well.

Apparently, in this town, your choices were limited. You either got the standard three-bedroom white cape with the black shutters and a black front door, or the standard three-bedroom white cape with the black shutters and a black front door. Even the flower beds looked the same, artistically curved around the base of each mailbox, each one planted with the exact same shade of nearly dead yellow and burnt-orange flowers.

Stripping off my gloves, I blew hot air into my hands. The houses lining the streets didn't exactly make me feel warm and fuzzy inside. In fact, they had me wondering what kind of dull, repressed people lived here.

Something about this whole neighborhood felt wrong. Horribly wrong. My senses hadn't been this jacked up in years. Not since that first night in the group home when I realized the girl bunking below me kept a makeshift knife tucked into the springs of her mattress. I'd spent my entire two-week stint there trying to avoid falling asleep, and I had a distinct feeling that if we didn't get out of here soon, I'd spend tonight doing the exact same thing.

"Holy house farm. They even have the same landscaping, right down to the flowerpot on the front step," Luke said.

"You think we'll get lucky and find a house key under one of those pots?" Mike asked.

"From the looks of it, I bet one damn key opens every house," I replied.

"Probably right. Let's go to that first one. I'm already halfway to hypothermia here," Mike suggested, only pausing when he noticed Luke counting the houses. "No. Don't even go there."

"House number three. We need to go to house number three." Luke grinned at me, no doubt preparing to take another verbal lashing over his idiotic fascination with triples. He played both football and lacrosse and insisted his uniform number be three. He'd applied to three colleges, and each one had to be within three hundred miles of home. He was even born on March third.

"Oh God," I sighed, dropping my head into my hands. "Here we go again."

"Hell no," Mike said. "We're going to the one right there." He pointed to the house closest to us. "Screw your lucky number obsession. I can't feel my legs anymore, and my nuts are already the size of raisins."

Luke smirked, undeterred by his brother. "It's not an obsession. It's lucky. I won big on it last week!"

I held my hand up to stop him. "That was a pee wee football ticket you bought from your cousin, and you won two tickets to a movie we'd already seen."

I was only half joking about my annoyance. The fact was, Luke had always favored the number three. Last spring he had it tattooed onto his middle finger. He claimed it was his own personal lucky charm. I'd laughed and told him *I* was supposed to be his lucky charm. I smiled whenever I thought about that tattoo, knowing full well he didn't choose that finger randomly. And I was fine with his little obsession back home, when it meant nothing more than watching the third movie in our Netflix queue rather than the first.

"Come on, guys. It's not like I'm asking for much," Luke said. He kissed my cheek, his dark eyes begging me to approve. "It's just two houses farther; we can see it from here. Plus, I've got a good feeling about this."

"Fine," I mumbled. "But if I end up with frostbite because of this, you aren't getting any for a month."

"Fair enough," Luke said as he came up beside me. "And I promise, Dee, I'll make it up to you later."

I grumbled under my breath. His hushed words left little to the imagination. Usually that tone would have left me feeling warm and buzzed, looking to ditch his brother at the nearest curb, but not tonight. Tonight was quickly turning into one giant bag of suck, and thoughts of being alone with Luke had died the second we hit that cemetery. There's nothing like the heel of your shoe sinking into a freshly dug grave to ruin the mood.

"Well, here we are," Mike said as we approached Luke's chosen house. "Should we try knocking?"

I took two more steps forward before I realized that Mike and I were alone. Luke was still standing at the curb, staring at the mailbox. "What's wrong?" I asked.

He shook his head, and I followed his eyes to the side of

the mailbox. The number seven was plastered on the otherwise unadorned piece of tin. I knew what Luke was thinking, but the agony of the cold was settling into my bones and every muscle in my body was beginning to ache.

"Ah ... yeah ... no. Third house. That was the deal. I don't care if it's number seven or number three hundred and thirty-three. If we don't find a phone or some gas, then we won't see any of it," I said, my mind still clinging to the futile hope that we would make at least the last set of the concert.

"See any of what?" Luke asked.

"Nothing," I said. There was virtually zero chance we'd make it to the concert, but I wanted to at least make use of the hotel room. "Let's hope somebody's home."

Mike rang the doorbell. When nobody answered, he put his ear to the door, listening for footsteps. Stepping back, he rapped his knuckles against the wood again and waited. "I don't hear anything," he said. "So much for your *lucky* number three."

Luke grumbled something about the number seven and shoved Mike out of the way. He reached for the doorknob and twisted it gently. I held my breath, expecting to hear the catch of a lock at any moment, but it never came. One click later, the door swung open, a hazy light falling across us from inside.

"Look, they were expecting us," Mike joked, waving me in. "They left the door unlocked and everything."

"Are you insane?" I hissed, not moving. "We can't just walk in. That's breaking and entering for real."

"No one's home, Dee. And if they are, once we tell them we're looking for a phone and some gas, they aren't gonna call the cops," Luke said. "Think about it. If we were running around their house with sacks full of their stuff, maybe. But not three kids looking for some help."

I studied Luke's expression, watching his eyes for any sign of doubt, but I saw none. I'd heard the intensity in his voice and knew full well that he wouldn't have suggested this if he hadn't thought it through a billion times. He was that type of person—the kind who formulated a backup plan for his backup plan.

Look at me, Dee," Mike said as he waved his arms around wildly, dozens of crystallized pellets sticking to the sleeves of his shirt. "It's freezing out here. Besides, Luke's right. We'll use the phone, wait for the tow truck to come pick us up, then be on our way. They won't even know we were here."

"This is crazy," I said, exhaling loudly. Taking chances wasn't something I was good at, and the thought of wandering into this house felt about as wrong as anything had in a while. "Fine, but only because we're out of choices. And if I hear anything, *anything*, then we're leaving. There's something screwy about this place."

I bit down on the inside of my cheek, silently cursing myself for getting us into this mess. On an ordinary Friday night I'd be at home, waiting for Luke to come watch a movie and trying to ignore the smell of Mrs. Hooper's not-yet-perfected veggie lasagna. Right about now, even that smell was appealing.

FIVE

A cold slap of air hit me the second I stepped through the door, the quick chill pushing me back outside rather than drawing me into the safe, dry confines of the house. Luke must have felt it too because he swept his arm backward, tucking me safely behind him. I wasn't complaining. I was more than happy to let Luke be the first one through that door.

The breeze quickly died, and the fluttering curtains went still. Mike pushed past me and was ahead of Luke in two strides. "Door," he said.

I stood there, silent, with no clue whether I should back out or come in and lock the door behind me. It wasn't until Mike started walking down the hall that I realized what he'd meant. The entryway opened into a living room. There was a hallway beyond it leading straight to the kitchen and a back door. It was *that* door that was wide open. The shot of cold we'd felt was a cross-breeze created by our sudden entrance.

Mike put a finger to his lips, motioning for us to stay quiet as he shut the door.

"I doubt there's anybody home," Luke whispered into my ear. "But stay here and let me and Mike take a look around."

I dug myself farther into his side. I wasn't remotely interested in wandering around this house until we were certain it was empty. And I didn't want Luke to either. But he smiled and peeled me off him, then motioned for me to stay put as he headed for the stairs.

Mike returned first, the ease of his stride letting me know he'd found nothing. "I walked around back," he said as he triple-checked the lock on the front door. "Nobody's out there. My guess is they left in a hurry when the sirens went off."

As much as I wanted to believe it was the sirens that had driven the owners away, the logic of that theory couldn't compete with my paranoia. "Or maybe they left when they heard us coming," I said.

Mike shrugged. "Doubt it. They've been gone for a while. If they'd just left, I'm pretty sure I would've seen them out there, but there's nothing but miles of fields. Plus, there's snow on the ground. I'd see their tracks if they left recently, and there aren't any."

I looked out the front window, searching what I could see of the neighbors' yards. Nothing but a clean slate of snow marred by *our* footprints

"Where's Luke?" Mike asked.

I lifted my chin toward the ceiling. I could hear Luke

moving around upstairs, the creak of the floorboards and the sound of doors opening and closing keeping me on edge.

"I'll check the upstairs with him. Yell if you need us," Mike said.

I stood there alone, listening to Mike and Luke's footsteps above. Their voices were muffled by the ceiling that separated us, but I could make out a few words. Luke laughed, that low rumble of amusement that only Mike could draw out, and I instantly relaxed. If Mike was joking and Luke was laughing, then things couldn't be that bad.

The heat clicked on, the soft whine of a furnace finally taking the chill out of the air. It was then, when my mind and body finally eased into the warmth pouring from the vents, that I looked around. I was standing in the living room. A very dull, very boring living room. The walls, the couch, even the curtains were beige. There wasn't a single picture on the wall or knick-knack on the mantle. In fact, with the exception of the dying yellow embers in the fireplace, the sole color in the room came from the massive gold cross hanging above the mantle.

I couldn't help myself. I reached up and touched the bottom of the cross. It was cool despite the fire burning below it. Even the Hoopers, the most religious people I knew—who went to church on Sundays and said grace before holiday meals—even *they* didn't having something this big hanging on their wall.

Drawn to the warmth of the fire, I found myself lingering there, peeling off my gloves as I tried to absorb the heat. I kicked off my shoes and wiggled my toes in front of the flames until I felt the soft, painful tingle of life returning. Once my body no longer burned with cold, I'd be able to focus on the moment and how we were going to get out of this place.

"All clear upstairs," Luke said, and I jumped at the sound of his voice, nearly toppling into the brick hearth as I spun around to see him. He reached out to steady me as Mike pulled back the screen and tossed in another log. The fire crackled, the embers suffocating under the weight of the new wood for a moment before flaring back to life.

"You find a phone?" I asked.

Luke shook his head. "I didn't see one upstairs. Let's check the kitchen."

I stripped off my damp socks and laid them out by the fire to dry. No way was I staying here more than a few minutes, but even that could make the difference between my feet being wet or numb. I stepped around the corner, skidding to a stop as I took in the kitchen. The table was set, and something had boiled over on the stove. From the looks of it, they'd been getting ready to eat dinner when whatever drove them away came knocking.

"Like I told you, someone left in a hurry," Mike said as he tossed the offending pot into the sink.

I glanced into the bottom of the pot, the brown, crusted mess on it heightening my fears. The weather may have been nasty, but not emergency-evacuation worthy. And definitely not bad enough to leave food unattended on a lit stove.

I turned back to the table and counted the number of plates. Three. Three sets of silverware. Three bowls of salad. Three glasses of milk. The napkins were tossed onto the plates and the bottle of salad dressing was tipped over, its contents pooling onto the nearest place mat.

Not thinking, I went over to the table and picked up the bottle. I used one of the napkins to clean up the mess before putting the salad dressing back in the fridge. I was planning to do the same to the butter and grated cheese when Luke caught my wrist and spun me around to face him. "Leave it, Dee."

I yanked my wrist free, a brief flash of panic forcing me to push him away. I rarely reacted to Luke like that, hardly ever let my past override what I knew to be the truth. But here in this house, in this town, nothing felt right.

Luke held up his hands, the look on his face clearly indicating that my reaction stung. "Dee, I would never—"

I waved him off, unwilling to allow my issues to make the night any worse than it already was. Truth was, I trusted Luke completely. I knew he wouldn't hurt me. Ever.

"Sorry," I muttered.

Luke nodded, but he kept his distance as I started clearing the table again. It was a monotonous task, something dull and rote to keep my mind off the inevitable. We'd missed the concert, it was freezing outside, and the quick look I'd had of this house told me there was no phone, never mind people. And we were stuck here.

"There's no phone," I mumbled as I dumped the milk down the drain. I quickly circled the kitchen in search of the dishwasher. There wasn't one. Of course not. Why would there be. "There's no dishwasher. I bet they don't even have a TV or a computer."

Mike nodded, confirming my thoughts. I sat down right

there on the kitchen floor, pissed that the night had been ruined, angry with myself for not checking the gas gauge, and more than a tiny bit scared. I hated feeling like this...like I had no control and absolutely no say in what happened next.

"It's no biggie," Luke said as he slid down in front of me and raised my chin so I'd meet his eyes. "We'll try another house."

That would be the logical solution, but my ability to reason had disappeared when I'd found myself playing hopscotch in a graveyard. "I don't get it. Who doesn't have a phone?"

"We don't," Mike said, and I glared up at him. I wasn't looking an answer. I just needed to vent.

"No, seriously, we don't," Mike continued. "We haven't had a land-line in almost two years. We only have cell phones."

I knew that, but I looked to Luke for confirmation anyway. "Yup," he said. "Mom had it disconnected. Said it was useless with how much we were on our cells."

The Hoopers had a land-line, one of those old things still attached to the wall. But they could barely figure out how to work voicemail, never mind learn how to text. Them having a wall phone made sense. The rest of the world...not so much. "So what are the chances any of these other houses have a phone?" I asked.

Luke shrugged, that familiar twitch of his shoulders that meant our odds weren't good.

"Okay, then let's go back to the car," I suggested. "We can flag down the next person who drives by."

"I know it seems safer there, but without gas, Dee,

we can't turn the heat on. That car is nothing but a metal icebox now."

"Then let's head back into town," I said. The house we were holed up in may have been warm, and there was plenty of food already on the table, but something about it freaked me out. "We can stay at that gas station until one of the attendants comes back."

It was Mike who answered this time. He went over to the picture window and drew back the curtains so I could see for myself. "It's dark out, and the wind is picking up. My guess is the snow isn't going to let up for a while, and the last thing we need is to get lost out there."

I knew what he was thinking. It was the smart thing to do, the safe thing, but that didn't make it any less horrifying. "What? You think we should stay here? In somebody else's house? All night?"

Neither of them spoke, and that was answer enough. "No," I said, looking at my watch. "It's barely seven. We have plenty of time."

"No we don't," Mike said.

"But what if they come home? I mean, they aren't going to be too happy when—"

"We already locked the doors," Luke said, cutting me off.

My eyes trailed to the front door. Not only had they locked it, but Luke had jammed a chair up against the handle. "What's that for?"

"Nothing," Mike said. "We just want fair warning should this town come back to life."

I thought Mike's choice of words was interesting and

almost asked him to explain what, *exactly*, he meant by "fair warning." But to be honest, I didn't want to know. Years of zombie movies had warped me, conditioned me to expect moaning throngs of rotting flesh in circumstances like this. And based on the primitive quality of the local cemetery, the dead wouldn't have far to crawl to get above ground.

"Fine. Whatever," I said as I made my way back to the fire. Heat or no heat, I didn't want to be here, didn't want to spend ten more minutes in this creep-show house, never mind an entire night. "But as soon as the sun comes up, we're leaving."

SIX

I was lying on the couch with my head in Luke's lap, staring at the front door and waiting for whoever lived here to come back home. The first trickle of true fear had finally settled like a living, breathing hum in my body.

"Tell me what you had planned for tonight," Luke said, and I didn't have to look up to see his forced smile; it rang clear in his voice. I doubted he really cared about our plans. Rather, he was trying to draw me out of my silence.

"Concert. I got third-row seats to see Mindhole. It was supposed to be an anniversary present," I said. "Out of all the nights for things to go bad, it had to be this one."

"I don't think it's that bad," Luke said. "I've got you here snuggled into me."

His hand ran the same path across my back as it had for the last half-hour. It was meant to be soothing, but with the wind lashing at the windows and the icy snow pinging off the shutters, it made me more anxious.

"You know I love you, right?" he asked. "And you know I would never let anything hurt you. Mike either?"

"Yes," I whispered. I knew that. Some days it was the *only* thing I knew, the only thing I could depend on.

"Then relax, Dee. I promise you're safe here with me."

Luke kissed the top of my head, his lips lingering there before moving to my cheek. "If it was supposed to be an anniversary present, then why did you bring Mike?"

I snorted at his attempt to change the subject. "I kinda needed his help with your parents. Lying to Mrs. Hooper was bad enough, but your parents... well, once I got in front of them, I could barely remember what I was supposed to say."

I chuckled, remembering the one fumbling attempt I'd made before breaking down and recruiting Mike for the job. I'd seen Mike lie to teachers about homework he'd forgotten and get out of a dates with a girls he'd accidently asked out when he was drunk. Mike could dance around the truth better than anybody, and, unfortunately for me, I'd needed his skill to pull this off.

Granted, it meant I had to be willing to put up with him all weekend, but if anyone could construct a web of lies without casting suspicion, it was Mike.

"His price for lying to your parents was a concert ticket," I said, leaving out the fact that I'd paid for Mike's room, his food, and the weed he'd insisted on scoring for the trip. No point in bringing that up, not when Luke was clearly trying to lighten my mood.

Luke groaned and mumbled something under his breath. I didn't catch much of it, just the vague promise that he'd make Mike pay.

I sat up and let my hands drop between my knees as I took another quick survey of the room. Mike was still in the bathroom. He'd spent the last ten minutes digging through the cabinets looking for contact lens solution. His was in the car. Even if he could get to it, it was probably frozen solid.

"This sucks." I couldn't help but feel responsible for the way things had turned out. Mike had originally suggested I forget the whole anniversary-concert-weekend-away thing and have a party with Luke's friends. He thought we should take the money I'd saved up and bribe his older cousin to get us a keg. I'd brushed off his suggestion and told him I wasn't interested in spending every last dime I had paying for Luke's friends to get wasted. I wanted to spend time alone with Luke, not cleaning up after his friends. Besides, some stupid Friday night party wasn't good enough. Luke deserved something better.

I hated to admit it, but I was beginning to think Mike was right. We should've stayed home and gotten a keg.

"If I'd gone with Mike's suggestion, then we wouldn't be stuck here."

"And what did Mike's plans involve? Beer and a crap-load of his friends?"

"Pretty much," I said as I ran a hand across the couch cushion. It was stiff and completely stain-free. Not a pulled thread or worn spot in sight. My eyes traveled to the end table—completely devoid of family pictures—and then to the

49

drab windows. There were no fancy fabrics or colorful patterns, only plain, old, white curtains. Nothing but perfectly boring symmetry everywhere you looked. If these people had any sort of life, you couldn't tell.

"It's not your fault, Dee."

"It *is* my fault," I said. The realization of exactly how screwed we were was finally settling in. "No one is going to notice we're missing until Sunday night."

"What do you mean, 'Sunday night'? Is that what you told my parents?"

"Not me. Mike," I said, the first tears beginning to pool in my eyes. "I told Mrs. Hooper I was staying at Dawn's house for the weekend, working on a Spanish project. Your mom thinks you guys are at Syracuse for some early admittance football thing where you meet the team and they try to convince you that Syracuse is your best choice."

Luke raked a hand through his hair, a character trait that usually meant he was pissed. Not at me necessarily, but pissed nonetheless. "And she believed that? Syracuse is on the bottom of my list."

I groaned, fighting the urge to look out the window for the hundredth time. We had no clue where we were. No one knew we were here. And this house wigged me out.

No matter how you slice it, this sucked.

SEVEN

It was still dark when I woke up. The fire had died out, and the house was totally silent. It wasn't noise or even my own fear that had startled me awake, just the soft dip in the couch cushion next to me. At first I didn't realize where I was, but eventually reality came rushing back. I shot up, the blanket covering me falling to the floor as my body instinctively went into a defensive posture.

"Easy, Dee. It's me," Luke whispered.

It took a minute for the voice to register and my body to relax. Once it did, I threw my arms around him, grateful that it was Luke and not some psycho-nut with a meat cleaver.

I pulled back quickly, gasping as cold water seeped through my shirt.

"Sorry," Luke said, shrugging off his coat.

"Why do you have your coat on, and why are you wet?" I asked.

I craned my neck to see the front door, sighing in relief when I saw the chair still propped beneath the handle and the lock firmly in place. I glanced back at Luke, confused. There were drops of water on his coat and his cheeks were red. He'd gone somewhere. Luke had waited until Mike and I had dozed off, and then that stubborn, stupid boyfriend of mine had gone outside.

"You went outside? Are you insane? What the hell were you thinking?" I yelled.

Mike woke up, grumbling something about me making too much noise before rolling over and settling back into the floor by the fire. I reached over and yanked his arm. "Luke left the house. Alone!"

Mike glanced at Luke. "Did you honestly expect him not to? He was pacing the floor half the night trying to figure a way out of here. Besides, it's not like we were making any progress sitting here."

Irritated that Mike wouldn't take my side, I turned on Luke. "You could've gotten lost or frozen to death."

Luke shook his head. "Nah. I was completely safe. I walked to the other houses on this street and checked to see if anyone was home. Nothing dangerous, I swear."

I sat there, torn between anger and pride. It was incredibly stupid, but deep down, I knew he'd done it for me. Luke got how much I hated this place, how I'd fidgeted for the first couple hours, unable to let my mind calm down enough to sleep. Plus, a tiny piece of me liked that he'd gone out looking for help. It was nice to have someone looking out for me, to feel like I wasn't completely on my own.

"Did you at least find a phone or some gas?" I asked.

"Nope, and I searched everywhere. I mean *everywhere*. No land-lines, no cell phones, not even a charger still plugged into a wall."

Mike wiped the sleep from his eyes and gestured at a pile of books on the floor. "What are those?"

Luke shot him a look—a pissed-off, *now-is-not-the-time* look that immediately put me on edge. "Nothing."

I looked at the six leatherbound books. Books that Luke obviously felt were important enough to drag back here. "That's a whole lot of nothing," I said. "What are they?"

Luke sighed and kicked the books out of my reach. "I don't know for sure. I didn't read them cover to cover, but my guess is they're some kind of manual. Every house I went into had one stored in the exact same place."

I heard the crack in his voice, the one that told me he was anxious and that there was more to these books than he was letting on.

"Manual for what?" I reached out and snatched one from the pile, dodging his hands as he tried to get in my way. I read the title out loud, tracing the letters as I spoke: "'Fashioning Children in the Image of God.'"

"Dee, wait. I don't think it's a good idea—" Luke's voice was desperate and frustrated as he begged me to drop the book. I ignored him and opened it to some random page, curious about what he was hiding.

The book was well worn, the pages creased and spotted

with dirt. My eyes raced over the words as my mind slowly struggled to comprehend what I was reading. I could feel the blood draining from my face, my hands shaking in time with each sentence I muttered.

The "board of education," which appeared to be nothing more than a long, wooden paddle, was used to align a child's thoughts with the teaching of scripture. Breaking the child's will was a gift, the red welts seen as a blessing… "a deliverance from evil."

I read farther down, wincing as the book graphically depicted how and where the blows were to be delivered and the number of strikes "reasonable" for the child's age. Stripped naked, their body was to be bared to the congregation; their punishment was to take place in public for the approval of witnesses. One strike for a child over the age of twelve months; ten for a girl over the age of twelve.

The book fell from my hands as images flooded my mind. I knew how it felt to be beaten with a wooden spoon, a fist, a belt. Those were memories that never went away. Regardless of time and no matter how much security Luke and the Hoopers offered me, those bits of my past were always there. And this book was bringing them all back.

EIGHT

"Every house has one?" I asked, and Luke nodded. "Where?"

"Kitchen. First drawer on the left," he said.

I flew off the couch, tripping over Luke's feet. He reached out to steady me, and I flinched. Being sheltered was the last thing I wanted. I wanted confirmation, proof that this town was as messed up as I thought it was.

I yanked the drawer opened and grabbed the book. The same worn cover, same emblazoned title staring up at me. I opened it, trying to find the page I'd just read. I missed—but not by much—and had to scan the next dozen pages before I found the chapter I was looking for.

This one had notes. The name "Joseph" was handwritten in the margin with dates scribbled next to it, each one referencing a specific punishment. Three lashings for not bowing his head during the blessing of the meal. Five for coughing during Sunday services. Eight for wetting the bed when he was six. They'd gone so far as to count the bruises and mark them down like tallies on a score sheet. The more bruises, the bigger the welts, the more favor you were shown from God.

I went to turn the page, mumbling about the other medieval forms of discipline outlined, when Luke snagged the book from my hand and tossed it back into the drawer. "Trust me, Dee. You don't want to read that."

"Did you?" I asked.

Luke's hand was fixed on the drawer, his fingers tightly clenched against the knob as if it might open on its own. "I read enough to know it's not good."

"Why didn't you wake us up the minute you found these? We could have left right then, been miles from here already," I said, wondering why he'd bothered to waste time reading the damn thing.

"It's dark out, Dee. Call me crazy, but in the light of day I can see what's coming at me."

That fact that he thought something would be coming at him—at us—was messed up and completely in line with my own fears.

I looked up at the ceiling and tried to imagine the kid who lived here. The one who'd been beaten. There were three bedrooms upstairs, or so I'd been told. Luke and Mike had searched them last night. They'd insisted there was nothing upstairs but some beds, and that it was as sparse as the main floor. Now, for some insane reason, I needed to see for myself.

I ran up the stairs, taking them two at a time. Mike and

Luke were behind me, each hurling their own set of questions in my direction. Yes, it mattered what was upstairs, and no, I wouldn't feel better leaving well enough alone. Ignoring their pleas to stop, I headed for the first room on the left.

Luke was right; this room contained nothing but the basics. There was a large bed in the middle with a white quilt covering it. A cane-backed chair sat next to the nightstand, and a pine bureau rested against the far wall. It was bare, not so much as a lamp or a bottle of perfume sitting on it. Even the mirror that should've hung above it was missing, replaced with a giant wooden cross. These people weren't simply religious, they were zealots.

Luke came up behind me and placed his hand on my shoulder. "Slow down for a minute. What are you looking for?"

"Nothing," I said, walking farther into the room.

I opened the closet, half expecting a dead body to fall into my arms. Instead, I saw a row of perfectly ironed clothes and smelled the faint hint of bleach. Shoes lined the floor—four pairs, all the black, tie-up, dressy kind. I backed up to get a view of the wooden shelf above the clothing rod and caught a glint of something shiny. Standing on my tiptoes, I slid my hand across the shelf, hoping to ease it forward. Cursing, I pulled my hand away and brought my finger to my mouth, tasting blood. Whatever was up there was sharp.

"Let me see," Luke said, holding his hand out for mine.

"No, it's fine. Just get me whatever is up there."

Luke didn't have to stretch to reach the top shelf. He stood back to get a clear view, then grabbed it. He stared at the objects for a second before holding them out for me to see: a stack of shallow metal bowls and what looked like a scalpel. I eyed the razor-sharp knife nervously, then went for the bowls.

"What are these, dog food bowls?" I asked, wondering why somebody would store them with their clothes. From what I knew of the downstairs, there were plenty of other pantry-like closets to store them in. Plus, there was no sign of a dog. No toys, no food, not even a stray hair on the couch cushions.

Luke shrugged. "That'd be my guess."

"What about the knife?" I asked, curious to see how he was going to explain that away.

"Room looks freshly painted," Mike offered up. "Maybe they used it to get the paint off the windows."

I didn't smell paint—not downstairs, not up here—but okay. I took the bowls from Luke's hand and set them on the edge of the shelf, then gave them a quick shove to get them as close to their original position as possible. As for the blade, well, I'd let Luke figure out what to do with that.

"I want to check the other closets."

"We checked the rooms last night, including the closets," Mike said as I turned to close the closet door. "We checked under the beds too. There's nothing up here."

As the closet door clicked shut, the soft thump of wood on wood echoed through the room. I debated whether to reach for the knob again or run. Logic overrode my fear, and I eased the closet door back open. Three hooks lined the inside of the door. Two of them held coats, the sleeves of each hiding what rested on the hook between them.

Moving the coats aside, I saw a tiny piece of rawhide that held a slab of wood in place. I fingered the cord briefly before picking it up. It was heavy, polished, and beautifully crafted, but there was no mistaking what it was: a paddle. The same one mentioned in the book. The same one used on whatever kid was unlucky enough to live here.

I turned it over and saw the inscription. I read it once to myself, then again out loud:

> *I will warn you whom to fear: fear him who,*
> *after he has killed, has authority to cast into hell.*
> *—Luke 12:5.*

It wasn't the quote that scared me, but the name. *Luke.*

I let the paddle fall back into place and turned to Luke. "Did you find that yesterday?" I yelled. "Did you see *that* when you searched the closets?"

Mike stayed silent, his eyes looking everywhere but at me. Luke shrugged, and that was answer enough. They'd found it. Ten bucks said that was why Luke had searched the other houses. He'd left me asleep in this messed-up place so he could wander around and see if the other houses held the same bizarre stuff.

I shoved my way past Luke. I wanted to know what other things were hidden up here, see exactly what else they'd found and *not* told me about.

The other two bedrooms were nearly identical to the first.

The only difference was they both held twin beds instead of a full. Same frames, same pine bureaus, same insanely creepy cross hanging on the wall.

I checked the closet in the first room, making sure to inspect the inside of the door. No hooks on this one and hardly any clothes. Two pairs of pants and a handful of white shirts were all that hung in there. There weren't even any shoes.

Mike put out his hand to stop me as I moved to the last of the three bedrooms. "The closet in there is pretty much empty. Nothing but some clothes. I swear."

I shot him a glare, one that I hoped let him know how little I believed him. "Yeah right, Mike. Like the first one was? 'There's nothing there, Dee.' Sure, nothing but a surgical knife and a paddle used to beat kids. What are you going to tell me next? That the insane manual we found in the kitchen is nothing more than an overdue library book?"

Mike went to fire something back, but Luke cut him off. "Let it go, Mike. If she wants to check the rest of the closets, let her."

I turned back to Luke, a little bit of my anger easing as I saw the apology in his eyes. Like always, he'd only been trying to protect me. It hadn't worked, and now he'd let me take control, knowing full well that I needed to see for myself what we were dealing with.

I scanned the room, my gaze landing on a folded-up sheet of paper lying on the floor next to the dresser. Half of it was stuck behind the bureau, and I had to tug it free.

It was creased, as if it had been crumpled up and tossed

aside. I laid it on the dresser and smoothed it out. The paper was thick, and at the very top was a seal. A gold cross. I squinted to make out the tiny inscription: *Purity Springs. Est. 1856.* I kept reading, the fancy script making the letters more prominent. A few lines in and it became clear what it was—a death certificate, complete with a name, birth date, occupation, even marital status. What it lacked was a date of death.

I cringed when I saw the name, my mind flashing back to the book I'd found in the kitchen drawer. It was as if I still held it, could feel the worn pages in my hand, smell the ink and years of use pouring from its pages. The name—Joseph—was written in the margin of that book. That same name was written here, neatly typed on a half-completed death certificate.

I'd never seen an actual death certificate before, but my gut told me that most people didn't leave them lying around their house…in their bedroom of all places. "Who the hell is Joseph Hawkins?" I asked.

"Is that what I think it is?" Mike asked, snatching the paper from my hands. "And why isn't it dated? You think this guy's already dead?"

Luke leaned in and stared at the morbidly disturbing piece of paper. "I didn't see that last night. Honest, Dee, I didn't."

Didn't matter whether he'd seen it or not; it was there.

I inched backward, my stomach twisting as the first wave of bile rose in my throat. "We can't stay here. These people aren't right. I don't care if I have to walk two hundred miles to the next town, I'm not staying here."

I ran out of the room and down the stairs, not waiting to see if Luke and Mike were following me. Luke caught me on the bottom step and put his hand on my arm to silence my quickly rising panic. "Dee, wait."

"I'm not staying," I said, my voice cracking with fear. "I'm leaving. Now!"

"We weren't planning on staying," Mike said.

I turned toward Mike's voice. He had my shoes and socks in one hand and a worn brown coat I'd never seen before in the other. I shuddered at the thought of putting on that coat. I couldn't help but wonder who it belonged to, if the owner of that coat was on the giving or receiving end of discipline.

"I'm not wearing anything that belonged to these people," I said.

"The snow may have stopped, but it's colder than yesterday," Luke explained as he took the coat from Mike's hand and held it out for me to put on. "And we've got a long walk."

I yanked my shoes and socks from Mike's hand and jammed my feet into them. Mike's jacket was sitting by the front door, draped over a heating vent, sucking up warmth. I grabbed it and shoved my hands through the sleeves, then stepped outside into the early morning light. "If you're so worried about the cold, then you wear it."

NINE

Every foul word I knew hissed from my mouth as I struggled to regain my balance on the snow-covered walkway. Luke was right. It was freezing, and everything was as slippery as hell. And it was going to be a long, cold walk out of this town.

The front door slammed behind me and I kept walking, refusing to turn back. I had no intention of ever laying eyes on that house again.

"Dee, wait," Luke called after me. The skating sound of sneakers on ice-caked snow approached, and I slowed to a crawl. No matter how much I wanted to lash out, I wouldn't blame any of this on him.

"What?" I asked as I whirled around to face him.

Luke skidded in my direction, had to reach out and grip the mailbox in order to stop.

"At least slow down a little," he said. "The car is over a

mile out, and one of us is gonna break something if we're not careful."

"I'll take a broken leg over staying in this house any day," I fired back.

Mike reached out to stop me before I took off farther down the road. I yanked my arm away and sent myself sliding in every direction until I landed on my butt.

"We weren't supposed to be here," I yelled at everybody and nobody. "We should've been sitting in the hotel's hot tub debating what to order from room service."

"That's not the point, Dee," Luke said. "We're—"

"It's totally the point. If I—"

"Both of you shut up for a minute," Mike said, waving us to a stop. "Luke, did you hit *all* the houses on this street last night?"

"No, only five or six. Why?"

We followed Mike's gaze across the street. When we'd gotten here last night, it was getting dark and the town was more than empty—it was brutally silent. Now I could see what looked like footprints in the slushy snow, and despite the fact that the sun was slowly rising, every porch light on the street was turned on.

"Tell me you turned those on last night," I said to Luke. "Please tell me you forgot to turn them off after you searched the houses."

Luke shook his head, not bothering to even try and ease my fear.

"That means somebody's here. That somebody prob-ably knows *we're* here. That somebody turned those lights on even though it's already morning, just to make sure we know they're here," I said.

"Oh, not merely somebody. Trust me on that."

We turned in unison at the sound of the voice, our gaze landing on a shadowy figure rounding the corner of the house we'd spent the night in. He kept walking toward us, coming close enough that I could make out the top button on his grungy, khaki-colored pants. I looked up into his eyes, trying to read his intentions. But they were dark and empty, and, if I had to guess, not a day older than mine.

Luke stepped in front of me, shielding me from the boy's view. "You take one step closer and I'll kill you," he warned.

The kid threw up his hands, assuring us he meant no harm, but I wasn't buying it. "He's not alone," I whispered. I didn't see anybody with him, but I didn't have to see them to know we were being watched. I could feel eyes tracking our every move.

Mike caught what I said and took two steps back. He turned in a complete circle, then shook his head. He'd seen the same thing as me—absolutely nothing.

Luke put a hand on his brother's shoulder when Mike went to approach the boy. Mike shook him off, his eyes never leaving the kid's as he spoke. "Seriously, Luke? There are three of us and one of him."

I doubted that was the case, and after reading those few short passages in that book, I didn't believe that anybody in this town was completely harmless. Maybe last night I was fine with asking complete strangers for help, but not now.

Surrounded by vacant, phoneless houses and creepy manuals ... if we were smart, we'd cut our losses and run.

I gripped Luke's hand and jerked hard. There was something about the boy I didn't like, something that made me feel threatened. "I have a strange feeling about him, Luke. Please, can we go?"

"Are you kidding?" Mike argued. "He's the first person we've seen, and I have some questions I want answered."

"I'm with Dee," Luke said, lowering his voice to a nearly inaudible level. "You have no clue what she's been through, Mike. None. Let me handle this."

I knew that's all Luke would say. It was an agreement we'd made last year when he'd begged me to tell him why I still flinched sometimes when he touched me. It had taken some prodding on his part, but I finally told him about my dad, the group homes, and the three foster families I'd lived with before finding the Hoopers. That night, Luke promised me that he would keep my past a secret and keep me safe.

Luke might have broken through my carefully fortified walls, but even now he still had to put up with a lot of my crap. He'd learned the hard way not to trap me against the lockers for a kiss and realized that tackling me on the bed to tickle me often landed him a knee to the balls instead of sex. But I was better now, or so everyone thought.

I watched Mike's expression darken as he processed Luke's words. It must've been hard to always be around me yet have no clue why I was so guarded, why Luke was so protective.

Luke took a step forward, a growl of warning rumbling from his chest.

The boy stood his ground, and my eyes traveled the full length of his body. The broad expanse of his shoulders, his height, and the size of his hands all gave me pause. He was *huge*. Not huge as in *one-too-many-pancakes-at-the-Waffle-House* huge, but huge as in *holy-crap-he's-built-like-a-brick-wall* huge.

Plus, there were a lot of pockets in his coat. And I'd learned a long time ago that pockets could hide a lot of weapons.

Luke scanned the horizon, no doubt looking for the boy's friends. His family. The rest of this town.

The kid nodded in understanding. "I'm alone."

"Who are you?" I asked.

He gave me a passing glance before ignoring my question. "Did Mary send you?"

"Who is Mary?"

He shook his head, his shoulders shrinking at my words. "Nobody."

"You have a name?" Luke asked.

"Joseph."

I knew that name. From the house. From the book. From the death certificate. "You're not dead."

He flinched as if my words somehow stung. He tried hard to cover it up, but I saw the panic flash across his expression. "Nope, not dead. Not yet anyway."

TEN

I spun around and gestured to the house we'd just left. "It's you. That's your house, isn't it? You're *that* Joseph."

His attention flicked over to the house, then back to me. It was quick, and I doubted Luke or Mike caught it, but I recognized it immediately—the fear and anger behind his expression, the quick flash of sorrow in response to a memory the rest of us didn't share. I recognized it because I'd mastered that same combination of emotions years ago.

The Joseph in the margin of that book, the one who got locked in the closet for six hours because he'd broken a dinner plate, was the same one standing in front of me now. He didn't need to admit it. The flat look in his eyes gave him away. And it was that look that worried me the most.

"It's you, isn't it?" I asked again, desperate to prove I was right.

When he didn't answer, I inched forward, intent on screaming my question at him. But he held up his hand and pressed a finger to his lips in a silencing gesture. In the absence of any sound, of any real people except for him and us, his gesture seemed odd.

"Why do we need to be quiet?" Mike asked, his head shaking in what seemed to be amusement. "In case you haven't noticed, there's nobody here."

"Oh, they're here. Trust me, they're here," Joseph said as his eyes met mine. He looked serious, so serious. And scared.

That makes two of us.

"What do you mean, 'they'?" I asked.

He ignored my question and fixed his gaze back on the empty road. "Listen. You've probably got an hour, two tops, to get out of here. After that, well ... "

"After that what?" Mike's tone was sharp, his normal carefree attitude slipping away, replaced by genuine anger. Luke nudged me back and rose to his full six-foot-two height, using all of his bulk to instill some well-deserved fear in Joseph.

I'd seen huge kids back away from Luke on the field, physically retreat from the defensive line. But Joseph didn't flinch; he met Luke's eyes without the slightest hesitation.

I leaned into Luke, standing on my tiptoes to whisper in his ear. "He lives there, Luke. That name in the book, on the death certificate. That's him."

"I know," Luke whispered, then raised his voice. "Listen, we don't want any trouble. We're just looking for some gas so we can get back on the road."

"That's going to be a problem," Joseph said, turning to

walk away. I guess he presumed we'd follow. He couldn't have been more wrong.

Luke reached out to grab him, his hand encircling Joseph's arm. "Where the hell are you going?"

Joseph stopped but didn't try and pull away. A shudder worked its way through his body. Maybe frustration. Maybe anger. When he finally turned around, his face was neutral, peaceful.

"My brother asked you a question," Mike started in. "And if it's all the same to you, I'd rather not stay in this place any longer than necessary. So, if you could point us in the right direction, that'd be fantastic."

Joseph smiled. "Brother, you say?"

"Uh huh. I'm Luke, this is Mike, and this is Dee," Luke said, pointing at each of us in turn.

"Dee," Joseph said as if testing my name. "Are you their sister?"

There was a twinge of hope in his voice, one that made me cringe. "Nope," I said, running my hand across Luke's waist before tucking it into the back pocket of his jeans. I wanted Joseph to know exactly who I was to Luke, who he'd have to go through to get to me. "I'm definitely *not* his sister."

Joseph looked at me, then at the hand I had tucked in Luke's jeans. "I'll help you. I can't get you gas, but I'll help you."

"Great," Luke said. "Start talking."

Joseph shook his head. "Not here. I'll tell you whatever you want to know, but not here. Not out in the open."

"Fine. There," Mike said, tipping his chin toward the

house we'd camped out in. "It's warm. I bet there's even some dinner left over from last night you could eat."

"No. No way. That's the first place he'll look."

I understood his hesitation. The house I'd grown up in was less than a ten-minute drive from the Hoopers', but you couldn't pay me to go back there. Not to the house. Not to the street. Not to the neighborhood.

I may have gotten the kid's mentality, but I was the only one. Luke had hit his threshold, his hand flexing in a useless attempt to rein in his anger. "Fine, then you stay here and do whatever it is this town does. We're leaving."

"You won't make it out of here," Joseph warned. "My guess is he's already found your car."

Done. That was the only way to describe Luke. Completely and totally done with Joseph. With this town. With this entire situation. "What the hell are you talking about?" Luke yelled, his entire body shaking in time with his anger. "I don't have time for this. Or you!"

I reached for Luke's arm, tugging on it until he made eye contact with me. The fire in his eyes quickly drained away, regret filtering in. He was scaring me, and he knew it. If the one person I counted on to be steady and strong was losing control, then things couldn't be good.

Luke looked back at Joseph and nodded his apology. "We're not going anywhere. Not until we have some answers, anyway."

"Fine, we'll play this your way," Joseph said. "Those sirens you heard, I set them off. That house you stayed in, that's mine. That grave you got your foot stuck in yesterday, that's my mother's. The man who put her there is named Elijah Hawkins. He's my father. And as for your car, well, that's not going anywhere."

"Your father?" I asked. My hands were shaking, my voice a strangled whisper.

Luke instantly reacted, wrapping his hand around my shoulder and pulling me into his side. I don't know what he whispered into my ear; I wasn't paying attention, but I knew from his tone that it was meant to be reassuring. It wasn't.

I closed my eyes tight, the hammering of my heart suddenly drowning out everything around me. We were at his mercy, this Joseph kid who'd come out of nowhere. This boy whose blank look haunted me like each bruise my father had left behind. He may have been my age, and we both may have suffered a broken arm or two courtesy of our fathers, but this kid was nothing, *nothing*, like me.

"What are you not telling us?" I mumbled.

"It's not easy to explain," Joseph said, and I squeezed Luke's hand, a billion horrible thoughts racing through my mind. Inbred townspeople. Radioactive mutations. Axe-wielding nut jobs. The possibilities were endless and insanely idiotic.

"Try," Mike said. "Because I want to know exactly what you meant when you said our car's 'not going anywhere.'"

"The car is the least of your problems," Joseph replied. "But if you can trust me for five minutes, I'll show you."

ELEVEN

We followed Joseph, not because we were stupid or we'd suddenly decided to trust him. We did it because we needed answers, and following him seemed like the only way to get them.

We cut through the backyard of his house and skirted the edge of the dying fields before Joseph led us into the stalks. I think he intended to hide our movements in the fields, which meant I had to trust that whatever lay on the other side of the decaying stalks was friendly.

On the surface, it made sense, but I was having no part of it. I needed a clear view not only of him, but of the town I feared would come roaring back to life. Luke's fascination with D-list movies had taught me well. I'd take my chances with the silent town rather than risk dancing with some machete-wielding nutcase.

I stopped dead in my tracks, Luke coming to a halt beside me. "I can't see the road if we're walking through the fields. I want to see the road."

"I agree," Luke said.

"There's a slight chance he doesn't know you're here yet," Joseph reasoned. "If that's true, you'd do best to keep it that way. I get that she's scared, and I have no intention of hurting her, of hurting any of you. I can help you, but you need to trust me on this. We need to stay clear of the road."

"Unless you got a can of gas or a speed pass out of this place, then there isn't a damn thing you can do to help us," Mike fired back.

"Gas is not what you need," Joseph mumbled, and I wondered what he meant by that. I planned on asking, but he started talking again before I got the chance. "Fine, we'll move closer to the road. We can cut a path three or four rows in. That should be close enough for you to see the street, but it'll give us enough cover that..."

"That what?" I wanted to know what was out there, what *he* was so afraid of.

"Nothing," Joseph said as the blank mask he was so fond of wearing settled back into place. "We should be fine."

We headed back toward the edge of the field. There were only three miserable rows of dying, waist-high stalks to conceal us. When the backside of the buildings started taking shape and I could make out the *closed* sign in a store's window, I relented and took a step farther into the fields. There was something about those darkened windows that had me wanting more than three feet of dead crops between me and them.

"You taking us back into town?" Luke asked. It wasn't a question; more of a subtle warning.

"No," Joseph replied.

"Then where?" Mike asked, obviously annoyed. "Cuz there's nothing but fields for miles. You can't tell me there's a phone booth or Holiday Inn sitting out in the middle of these stupid corn stalks."

"It's soybeans, not corn, and no, there's no ... " Joseph paused, waffling his hand as if he was trying to comprehend the meaning of the words "Holiday Inn." He eventually gave up and moved on to Luke's original question. "We're not going into town. We're headed toward an irrigation shed on the *edge* of town."

"Irrigation shed?" Luke questioned. "Yeah, no."

Joseph ignored him and kept walking, stopping abruptly a few yards up. His attention was focused on the town, and it took me a second to grasp what we were supposed to see. "I'm guessing that looks familiar," he said.

I stumbled back and landed on my butt for the second time that day. Luke went to help me up, fear clouding his eyes. He'd seen the same thing and was doing little to shield me from his panic. Joseph watched me carefully, his eyes softening briefly as I surveyed the crumpled-up hood of a car that looked alarmingly like ours.

I needed to get a lot closer to confirm the license plate, but given that every other car in this town was your standard blue, four-door Ford and ours was a red Toyota, there was little left to guess. And it was sitting right there in the gas station lot. Town still deserted. Streets still silent. But our car had been moved, towed to the same station I'd begged Luke to let us hide out in last night.

The front driver's side of our car was bashed in, nearly totaled, and even from a distance I could see that the hood was popped open. My eyes trailed downward and I noticed what looked like a piece of the engine lying on the ground next to our flat front tires. Apparently Joseph was right. Finding gas was the least of our problems.

"That's our car," Mike said, his voice seething with anger. "What did you do to it and how did it get there?"

Luke fished around his pocket and pulled out the car keys, staring at them in disbelief. "What the hell?"

"I didn't do anything to it. I'm trying to stay hidden like you."

"Why should we believe you?" Mike fired back.

The time it took for Joseph to acknowledge the question seemed like forever. It was like he knew there was no possible way to convince Mike completely, so why bother to try.

"I don't know what you want me to say," Joseph finally replied. "I didn't do it, and I want out of this town as much as you. Probably more."

I exchanged glances with Mike, wondering if he'd buy Joseph's explanation. I doubted he would.

"There's no way we're following you into some shed," Luke said. "There is not a single person in this town, you destroyed our car, and don't even get me started on the weird shit we found in your house."

Rather than answer, Joseph tilted his head to the right, as if seeking out a sound that no one but him could hear. The stalks on our left swayed. Luke saw it too and we both swung our heads around, hoping to God we weren't surrounded.

In front of us was the town and God-knows-who. Behind us was the messed-up house I had no intention of ever setting foot in again. Whoever was parting those stalks to our left was also rapidly approaching from the right. And Joseph stood dead in front of us. None of our options looked good, and we didn't have the time for a debate. Whatever was coming out of those fields would be on top of us in seconds.

"Where's the shed?" I blurted out. I didn't want to go there any more than Luke did, but right then it seemed like the safest place to be.

"There." Joseph pointed, already running toward it. The small rectangular structure was half a field away; half a field for whatever was stalking us to speed up and catch us out in the open.

TWELVE

Since it consisted of little more than a roof over what appeared to be a gigantic motor and a mess of pipes, I couldn't
imagine this was the shed Joseph was referring to. A few
posts held the A-frame roof above the tangle of run-down
equipment. With only one wall at the back, it looked more
like a stall than anything else. I didn't see any space for a
body to fit, never mind four.

Luke stood at the edge of the massive motor, his lips
pressed into a thin, tight line. "What is that?"

I peered around him, inhaling sharply as a second shed
came into view. The water pump and irrigation equipment
had completely eclipsed my view of the even-smaller structure behind it.

This shed was about half the size of the shoebox dorm
room Luke complained about having to live in next year. And

with no idea who or what was waiting on the inside, I seriously considered taking my chances with whatever was out there in those fields.

"I don't think I can do this." I heard the panic in my own voice and glanced behind me, searching the fields for a sign that whatever had been lurking there was gone. "I changed my mind. I don't want to go in there."

Luke advanced on Joseph, his eyes filled with a protective anger. "I'm going to trust you because right now I don't have any other choice. But if you hurt her, if you so much as look at her funny, I'll kill you with my bare hands. You got that?"

"And I'm more than happy to help him," Mike added.

Joseph yanked back the heavy wooden door, his voice shaking, his hands trembling as he spoke. "I'm not looking for a fight. I just want to get inside the shed."

I stood completely immobile, staring at those hands. Big and calloused, they looked like they'd never seen a drop of lotion. The fingernails were short but jagged, and a variety of scars—some fresh, some healed over—blanketed his skin.

"What's in that shed that's so important to you?" I asked.

"Safety." Joseph paused before taking his first tentative step inside. He disappeared into the darkness and I leaned forward, straining to see or hear something... anything.

I heard the strike of a match seconds before I saw the flash of light, and my nose burned with the unmistakable smell of sulfur. Joseph's shape came into view, the light intensifying as he placed the glass globe onto the lantern and adjusted the wick. In that brief, unguarded second, I saw the defeat weighing him down. I didn't know if he was nuts or brave or stupid, but the one thing I could tell was that he was desperate.

"Nobody will come in here. We're safe," Joseph said, coaxing us in. "But if it makes you feel better, there's a board over there in the corner you can wedge underneath the handle."

Mike eyed the board but made no move to retrieve it. I knew what he was thinking. That piece of wood could trap us in as easily as it could keep somebody out. I was with him; I wanted a quick escape should things go wrong.

Luke grabbed my hand and inched us backward out of Joseph's reach. "Hey," he whispered as he tried to gentle the death-grip I had on his hand. "Don't worry. Like Mike said, there are three of us and one of him."

"Sure," I mumbled. Spending an entire night in a stranger's house was messed up enough. Expecting me to walk into a dimly lit room with a kid we knew nothing about was too much.

"Is there any other light?" I asked.

"Nope, this is all I could get my hands on," Joseph said as he turned a knob on the base of the lantern, sending the flame flaring a bit higher. I could see the entire shed now. Mike was standing guard by the door, Joseph was sitting on the floor in the corner, and Luke was plastered to my side.

"We just left a neighborhood full of empty houses. Why didn't you grab a flashlight or another lantern?" Luke asked as he let go of my hand and took up a spot on the floor opposite Joseph.

"There's no way I could take anything without being noticed. He catalogs everything. *Everything.*"

My mind flashed back to last night. Had we eaten anything? Taken anything by accident? Left anything behind? I'd done the dishes, and I was quite sure we'd left the six copies of that disgusting book somewhere in that living room, along with our tire iron and flashlight. *Crap.*

Instinctively, I put my hand down and brushed the floor before sitting. Except for a thin layer of dirt and a few nails poking up from the floorboards, it was bare. There were no windows, no sources of light other than the lantern, and, from what I could see, the shed was completely empty—no tools, no equipment, not even a freaking chair to sit on.

For as small and empty as this shed was, it felt huge, each corner vibrating with a terrifying energy. "Why aren't there any tools in here?"

"Because it's not really a shed," Joseph replied.

"Then what the hell is it?" Luke asked as he picked up the lantern and raised it over his head. "Holy hell, what is that for?"

I looked up, my breath catching in my throat as my own reflection stared down at me. "What's with all the mirrors?"

I gestured for Luke to lift the lantern again and inspected the ceiling once more. The mirror ran the entire length of the shed from edge to edge, no seams. Nothing to break the reflection.

"Damn," Mike said as he stepped away from the door. He looked up, turning a full circle with a stupid smirk on his face. "Done right, this room could have some serious potential."

Joseph cocked his head, wondering what Mike was talking about. Luke grumbled for him to knock it off, and I kicked him. Mike swore, but he got the message and returned to his post by the door.

"My father calls this place 'The Livor.' A place for reflection." Joseph's voice changed, went softer as he recited something from memory. "'Now we see things imperfectly, like puzzling reflections in a mirror, but then we will see everything with perfect clarity.'"

I stared at him, my mind running through the few Sunday masses the Hoopers had talked me into attending. I didn't remember that verse. What I did remember was first-year Latin. I hadn't retained much of that dead language, but I knew for a fact that the term "livor" had absolutely nothing to do with reflection.

"Livor means punishment, not reflection," I said.

Joseph shrugged, as if he didn't understand the difference. "That mirror is for penance. To find yourself. This is where you go, where he sends you, when you're lost."

"Lost?" I asked, not following what he was saying.

"When you stray from the teachings," Joseph explained.

"That's . . . messed up," I said.

Luke wrapped his arm around my back as Mike cracked open the door. He peered out briefly before closing it, then turned his attention back to us. "All quiet," he said.

Joseph straightened up and moved over to where Luke was sitting. "Hold the lantern up again, toward the wall."

I followed the light's path. Hundreds of jagged scratches marred the walls, as if a wild animal had been turned loose in this tiny, confined space. I traced one with my index finger, drawing back suddenly as a sharp splinter of wood jabbed me.

"My father has a theory," Joseph started. "Before you can rebuild a man in God's image, you must break him down, strip him of his earthly sins so the blood of his soul can run pure. No one ever gets out until they're broken and reborn. It could take days, but without food or water, nobody lasts long."

He paused for a minute, his eyes glossing over. I didn't want to know where he'd gone or what memory he was reliving. With a visible shake, he brought himself back and continued. "There's no sound, no food, nothing to distract you. Only the image of yourself staring back at you. Eventually, you give in and tell him whatever he wants to hear, become whoever he wants you to be, just to get out."

Joseph took the lantern form Luke's hand and lowered it back to the floor. "Nobody ever comes here willingly. Trust me, this is the last place he'd think to look for us."

I turned my attention back to the ragged scratches, my mind filling with images of tiny kids screaming as they tried to get out. "Those marks are from people, aren't they? Like someone trying to claw their way out?"

Joseph wrung his hands tightly in front of him. "I've spent six full days in here, heard nothing but the irrigation motor, saw nothing my own reflection. Trust me, I came out saying whatever, doing whatever, and believing whatever I was told to."

Mike leaned into the light of the lantern, his face twisting in disbelief. "Are you for real?" He made eye contact with Luke, then me. "God, don't tell me you guys are buying any of this crap, because—"

Luke held up his hand, cutting Mike off. "It doesn't matter what he's selling, Mike. My only concern is how we're going to get out of here."

"Wait," I said waving both of them off. "You can't keep kids holed up in here for days. There are laws against that. I mean, I know there are..." I trailed off, not wanting to admit how I knew.

"According to my father, there's no law outside of his law...outside of God's law."

I clutched my stomach, afraid the nausea that was building was going to force me out of the shed and back into the open. I had to swallow twice to get my next words out. "I don't understand. If this is some kind of freaky solitary confinement, then why is it all the way out here where the adults can't see it?"

"It's safer out here. You know, in case an outsider passes through town. No one would hear or see anything. What happens here in Purity Springs stays here. Plus, the noise of the irrigation pumps drowns out the screams, and—"

"Wait," Luke interrupted. "People pass through?"

Joseph smiled, amused, it seemed, at the simplicity of Luke's revelation. "Yup. People stop here for gas all the time. They fill up and grab something to eat or drink, then move on. We need the money to keep the town running, and my father doesn't mind people passing through, as long as they pay for whatever they buy and keep going."

"Great," Mike drawled. "So what makes us so special? We'd be happy to pay for our gas and keep going. I'll slip him an extra fifty if that would help."

"He doesn't want your money, and he won't let you go. He thinks you're with me. He thinks you're the ones who tried to help my mom get out. That you're helping me now."

"But we're not. We weren't," I argued.

Joseph shuffled his feet, his eyes trained on the ground. "I know that, but you don't get it. Like I said, the only truth that matters in Purity Springs is his."

THIRTEEN

I finally grasped what this tiny, dark room actually was: a twisted way of sending a naughty child into the corner, complete with locks and sensory deprivation. What I didn't get was why Joseph hadn't left this place years ago.

"Why are you still here? You said you were hiding from him, and that your mom was trying to get out. Why haven't you run away?"

"It's not that easy. I grew up here. It's who I am," he answered.

I wasn't buying that. It took me twelve years to get out from under my dad's control, but I finally did. And I wasn't planning on stopping with the Hoopers. I was going to put as much distance between myself and my past as I could. I had college to look forward to . . . a place to start over with Luke.

"We don't have phones," he said. "And up until three

days ago, I had no idea what was past these fields. In fact, I'd been told—no, *warned*—not to go looking."

"I'm not following," I said, and from the look on Luke's face, he wasn't either.

"Everybody here can trace their roots back to one of ten original families. Nobody new moves in, and nobody born here ever leaves. That's how we keep our town pure, free of the evil that lives beyond."

"Ah, sorry, don't mean to interrupt your history lesson," Mike cut in. "But help me out here, because I'm a little hung up on that whole 'lives beyond' comment. *We* are what lives beyond. Us and about five billion other people who don't give a rat's ass about your little town."

"I believe you. My mom did too. That's why she was getting ready to leave. She wanted to take us with her. I was helping her. We had a plan and a place to stay. We were supposed to leave two days ago, but…"

"But what?" Mike's asked, his tone becoming more abrupt each time he spoke. "I don't see anybody stopping you. Get up and leave."

"I wouldn't get a half-mile from here before my father found me. Besides, I can't."

"You keep saying that," I yelled. "How do you know that? How do you know if you've never even tried?"

"Because I know what happens to people who try," Joseph replied. "My father caught my mother talking to some couple who stopped for gas last week. They had a map out. He got suspicious. Angry."

"Are you saying that your mom wasn't *allowed* to read

a map, to speak with someone who lives on the other side of your town-limits sign?" Luke asked.

"Technically, it's not a sign. It's the giant oak tree by the water tank twenty-two miles west of here. But yes, that's correct."

Joseph averted his gaze, focusing on a nail pulling loose from the floorboards. I could see the shame in his eyes, in the way his entire body curled in on itself. I wanted to know if his mom was asking for directions, if she was planning on escaping and that's what got her killed. "Was she asking for directions?"

He smiled at my question. "Yes. She had a sister on the outside. That's where we were heading. She was trying to figure out how to get there."

"Mary?" I asked, remembering the first words he'd spoken to me in the street.

"When I saw you, I thought . . . " He paused for a second, then shrugged. "I thought that maybe when we didn't show up at her house, she figured something was wrong and sent somebody . . . sent *you* to see what had happened."

I shook my head. "You said your father killed your mom. How? Why?" It didn't make any sense. Why would this Mary lady send help to someone who was already dead? Unless she didn't know . . .

"He wasn't trying to kill her, only bleed her," Joseph said, and we all stared at him in confusion. "Purify her. Release the evil. You know . . . bloodlet her."

"Are you kidding me?" Mike asked. He was standing closer now, glaring down at Joseph.

I grabbed Joseph's arm, my fingers digging into his skin. "If what you're saying is true, then why are you sitting here doing nothing? You need to head to the edge of town and keep walking. I mean, it doesn't get much easier than that."

Joseph looked at us, at *me,* with an intensity I couldn't read. "I can't."

I knew there was more to this than he was saying, but no matter how hard I tried, I couldn't get the pieces of his story to line up. No one would willingly stay here. No one.

"Can't or won't?" Luke asked, and for the first time I realized he'd been quiet for the better part of the conversation. But he had that gleam in his eyes, the one he got whenever he was watching the offensive line of an opposing team, trying to predict their next play from their formation alone. Luke was paying attention all right, probably more so than Mike or me.

"Won't," Joseph replied.

Luke studied him for a minute, his silence and scrutinizing stare making me nervous. Then he smirked, and I knew he'd draw some conclusion, picked up on something I'd missed. "What's her name?" he finally asked.

Joseph didn't answer immediately, and Luke grinned, convinced he'd pegged him right. "So? Her name?"

"Eden," Joseph whispered. "But it's not what you think."

"You have no idea what we think," I said. "But if your father is the maniac you're making him out to be, there's no way he's gonna let you walk back in there and take her with you."

"You don't get it," Joseph said. "I can't leave her."

"Sure you can," Mike piped in. "Trust me, there are plenty of other girls out there. I can even introduce you to some."

Luke and I both swung our heads in Mike's direction, more than a little disgusted. Luke would never leave me behind. *Never.* The fact that Mike would pissed me off.

Joseph shook his head, a grim acknowledgement that the answer to his problems was far more complicated than I was making it out to be. "It's not like that. Eden is my sister, and I won't leave her behind. I promised my mother I'd keep her safe, that if her plan didn't work, I'd find some way to get Eden out of Purity Springs. And that's what I'm going to do."

I got what he was saying. I was lucky enough to be an only child. One less person in this world for my father to beat up on. One less person for my mom to abandon. But if I had a sister ... well, I'd like to think I wouldn't leave her behind either.

"Does Eden know what your father did?" I asked.

He shrugged and turned away. I could feel the guilt pouring off him like a live wire. "I was there when he bled my mom. I begged him to stop, told him he was going too far. When she died, he pulled the town together, told them that his 'sacrifice' was for the greater good. *His* sacrifice. *HIS.* My mother is dead, and somehow he's managed to convince the entire town that her death was necessary. That it couldn't be stopped."

"What did you do?" I asked, wondering whether he'd stood up to his father in public, told everybody in this town the truth about what had happened.

"Nothing," Joseph replied. "I lost it and ran."

I got the running part. What I didn't get was why he'd stopped. I knew he wanted to save his sister and all, but at some point you gotta recognize your limitations. If this guy was truly the monster Joseph was describing, then he couldn't do this alone.

I suddenly realized that Joseph knew that. I realized it was why we were here, camped out in the shed, staring at clawed walls and mirrored ceilings. He wanted, no, he *needed* our help.

"I've been watching outsiders pass through this town since I was born, and never once did they pose any threat or inflict any harm. They got what they needed and moved on. But my father told me not to be fooled, that the devil had two faces—one charming and meant to draw you in, the other full of sinful pride."

I looked from Luke to Mike, wondering if they were listening to the same crap as me. Mike looked amused; Luke had a blank stare of disbelief covering his face.

"I made it three miles outside of town yesterday before I stopped and sat down, waiting for whatever evil lurks out there to find me," Joseph continued.

"And?" I prompted.

"And nothing. I sat there for three hours and didn't see anything but a few birds. Nothing evil. Nothing bad. *Nothing.*"

"He hasn't come looking for you yet?" Luke asked.

"Oh, he did. He's searching for me now."

I spun around, surveying the dimly lit room. I knew his father wasn't here. I knew the door was shut and Mike was standing in front of it. Whatever we'd seen outside the shed was gone, replaced by dead silence. But that didn't stop me from looking.

"And that's your problem, isn't it?" Mike said. "He knows you'll come back, that you won't leave without your sister. Your father has you by the balls and there isn't a damn thing you can do about it."

"Not alone. But with you, with all of us, maybe." Joseph cast a hopeful look in my direction, his eyes locking on mine. Somehow the kid had figured out that I got him, that I understood what he was going through. That shared knowledge scared the crap out of me.

Luke caught Joseph's look and moved forward, angling his body in front of mine. "Hell no," he barked. "You leave Dee out of this. Eden's your problem, not ours."

"It's not like I haven't tried to get her out on my own," Joseph said. "I did. I'm the one who set off the sirens. I tried to create a diversion so I could grab her and run. But my father wouldn't let her out of his sight. Now he's got the entire town holed up in the basement of the chapel. He'll keep them there until he gets a handle on the situation, until he can make sure the threat is gone."

I knew what he was getting at. We, and in some way Joseph himself, were the threat. And by "gone," I knew he didn't mean safely removed from his town. He meant the six-foot-under kind of gone. I felt bad for the kid, but I'd be insane to risk any of our lives for a stranger.

"I'm sorry," I said as I reached a hand out to him. "We can't help you. You can come with us, though. The next town we hit, we'll find the police, tell them what's going on. They'll come back here and get your sister out."

Joseph shook me off, not interested in my suggestion. "That could take hours. Days. I don't have days. Plus, no one in the next town is going to help me. You're my only chance to save her."

When none of us budged, he continued. "My mother was fourteen when she was forced to marry my father. Eden is twelve, and Elijah has three high-ranking followers who are in need of a wife. I overheard them talking—each of them was pleading his case, telling my father why he was the better choice for Eden."

I shook my head in horror. I knew what these men wanted from Eden. It was the reason why the state had finally taken me away from my father for good. My dad hadn't...but he'd tried. He'd been stumbling drunk and off-balance, giving me the...no, this was going to stop right now.

"There's no way, that's—no way—I—" I struggled to get my words out, then finally came up with a not-so-simple "No!"

Luke interrupted my rambling. I think he did it to shut me up and give me time to lock those memories away more than anything else. "Listen, man, I'm sorry. I really am. And our offer still stands. You can hike out of this town with us, but that's the best we can do."

I nodded in agreement and backed toward the door, hoping Joseph would follow our lead and leave this town behind him.

"Apparently I didn't make myself clear," Joseph said as he stood up. "I wasn't giving you a choice."

For some reason, he looked bigger, more threatening than before. Maybe it was the clarity of his voice, the pause between words as he carefully articulated each syllable. Joseph was no longer desperate or frustrated. His behavior was deliberate. Calculated. Either way, it had me backing into the wall out of his reach.

He didn't head toward Luke or Mike—he came straight at me. But he didn't get more than a half-step in my direction before Luke snapped, the fine thread of control he'd been holding onto breaking as he let loose with a violent string of curses.

"You don't touch her!" he screamed, lunging at Joseph. He hit him square in the chest, his hands going for Joseph's throat.

I don't know whether it was Luke's intention or just the sheer force of his weight, but he slammed Joseph into the door and it flew open, both of them stumbling out.

"Luke!" I screamed and ran after them, skidding to a stop as the sunlight blinded me.

A shadow of movement to my left caught my eye, the low growl of an unfamiliar voice breaking through the chaos. I vaguely registered Mike screaming, yelling at me to run.

A loud crack echoed through my mind, and I wondered if the ringing in my ears had anything to do with the dull pain creeping across the back of my head. My world spun, Luke's face going in and out of focus as I felt my cheek melting into the cold, wet ground.

The last thing I remembered, the last thing I heard, was Luke's voice and my name all muddled together into one ear-piercing jumble of words. Then everything went dark.

FOURTEEN

I swung my head to the left, trying uselessly to clear the sound that was dragging me back from the peaceful darkness. The rhythmic dripping of water echoed through the room, keeping me marginally aware when all I wanted to do was slip back into blissful unawareness. Something cool and damp slipped across my forehead. I tried to swipe it away, but my hands were too heavy to lift. Eventually, I gave in and let my head fall forward.

My stomach clenched with the movement. I forced my head up and searched the room for a focal point, something to concentrate on until my world stopped spinning. I found it—a small crack in the wall at the far corner of the room. That tiny spot became my anchor, and I used every ounce of energy I could muster to simply keep it in my sights.

I stayed still, a deep haze blanketing my mind. The corner of the room shifted in and out of focus, shadows of light dancing behind my eyelids each time they drifted closed. Blinking long and hard, I concentrated on that spot again, began to process the rough outlines of a cinderblock wall. I blinked again, and the whole wall came into view. With that came a flood of thoughts. All scattered. All useless.

It hurt to think, the mere effort driving me to the brink of tears. Gasping for breath, I squeezed my eyes shut as the pain flared through the back of my head. It lanced through my skull like a hot poker. Moisture seeped across my scalp and trickled down my neck. I harnessed what little strength I had and attempted to bring my hand to my head in hopes of dulling the pain, but I couldn't. My hand wouldn't move.

"What the…?" I peered through the darkness at my hands. They were strapped down. Thin white plastic was laced around my wrists, tethering me to a chair. I did what came naturally; I jerked against the restraints, ignoring the pain as they dug deeper into my skin.

I braced my feet against the floor, hoping to gain some leverage. *My feet. They weren't bound.* That knowledge coursed through me like a victory chant, and I dug my heels in to the cold tile and managed to lift all but my wrists off the chair. I winced through the pain and yanked harder. For all my efforts, the only thing I succeeded in doing was tipping over the chair.

Something—no, *someone*—caught me and gently eased the chair back upright.

"Shhh. Don't pull against those. You'll hurt yourself."

Joseph's voice was fuzzy, blending into the darkness somewhere beside me. I tried to zero in on his shadow, on the blurry image that was lingering around me, but I couldn't. Again, too painful.

"You sick bastard!" I pulled at the zip-ties again, deepening the already raw depression that circled my wrists. "What did you do to me? Where's Luke? Where's Mike?"

My shrieks echoed off of the walls as the room slowly materialized around me. It was bare except for what looked like a beat-up table, another chair, and an enormous gold cross hanging dead-center on the far wall.

A hand clamped down over my mouth, and I yanked my head from side to side in a useless attempt to free myself. As his fingers dug into the sides of my cheeks, I fought back the wave of tears that were building.

"You've got to relax and calm down, Dee. If you don't, he'll hear you and come in," Joseph soothed.

I wasn't going to calm down, and I'd be damned if I was going to sit here quietly. I nodded slowly so that he'd ease his grip, then bit him hard enough to draw blood.

"Sweet mother of—" Joseph swore, bringing his hand to his mouth to nurse his wound.

"Let me go," I begged. I was nauseated and could taste his blood in my mouth. On top of that, I couldn't seem to shake the sensation that I was wet, dripping from somewhere on my left arm. My head slipped backward and my neck felt rubbery, dense, as I tried to right it again.

"Hold still, Dee. You need to stay calm and trust me here."

Trust him? Was he kidding me?

"Why? What did you do to me?" My speech was slurred, each word becoming more and more difficult to force past my lips. Glancing down, I saw blood staining my forearms, trailing from the crook of my elbow onto the chair.

There were three cuts—none more than an inch long—on each arm. All oozing.

I stared at my right arm for a minute, hyper-focused on the muted sound of each drip as it hit the metal pan below. Then I lost it, covering myself with a fully digested round of stomach bile.

Joseph saw me heave and jerked out of the way.

There was a knife on the table, along with three murky glass jars containing what I assumed was my blood. In the back of my mind I knew what this was, knew this was how his mother had died. But that knowledge, no matter how heinous, couldn't compete with the exhaustion sweeping over me.

My head swayed as I tried to force myself to stay upright. "I got to stay awake," I mumbled, fearing that sleep was just the opportunity death needed. "Please, Joseph, don't let me fall asleep."

"You can sleep, Dee," Joseph said, his hand brushing a damp strand of hair off my forehead. "I'll be here watching you, and I promise I won't let anything bad happen."

He laid a damp cloth on the back of my neck, then wrung out another and gently wiped it across my face. He was cleaning me up. He'd tied me down, bled me, and now he was cleaning me up.

"Don't do this, Joseph. Please, let me go." My voice was a

whisper, so soft that I wondered if I'd only spoken the words in my mind.

"I'm not going to hurt you," he said as he slowly cleaned my wounds.

The sting of alcohol momentarily jarred me awake, and I flinched against his hand, trying to get him to leave me alone. It was useless; I was tied tighter than luggage to the top of a family car.

He let up on the alcohol and gently placed his hand over mine, calming me. "I won't let my father hurt you either. I promise you, Dee. That's why I'm here."

"Where's Luke? Where's Mike?" I asked again.

"Safe," he replied.

"Safe where?" If I could get an idea of where they were, then maybe I could get to them.

"Don't worry. They aren't here. They're still on the outside."

That was good. Somehow I knew that was good. I didn't want to be in here alone, but if Luke and Mike were on the outside, then there was a chance they could go for help. All I had to do was say alive.

"Why did you do this, Joseph? I would've helped you. I would have convinced Luke to . . ." I stopped and swallowed hard. The words were thicker now, almost impossible to formulate.

Joseph's outline shuffled in and out of my vision, his movements twisting around in my mind as my eyes fluttered closed. His voice was soft, gentle against the horrible soundtrack of my own blood gathering in the bowl beneath me.

"I'm sorry," he said.

I shook him off, the cold compress he was holding at the back of my neck falling to the floor. "Why? Tell me why."

"I need to get Eden out of here. She doesn't understand what my father has planned for her. She's too young, too innocent to break free on her own."

"We never said we wouldn't help—"

"I know what you said." Joseph cut me off. "I know I could've left with you and your friends. But it's not me I'm afraid for; it's Eden, and your friends made it clear they wouldn't risk coming back into town to help me save her. But I bet they'll come back for you."

The tears I'd been fighting finally gave way. Joseph was right. Luke may not have been willing to risk our lives to save a stranger, but he'd absolutely give his life to save mine.

The soft echo of footsteps filtered down the hall. I counted to five, then listened again, hoping to God the sound was nothing more than fear pulsing through my veins. But it was still there. And getting louder. Getting closer.

"Close your eyes," Joseph whispered.

I shook my head. I wanted to see Elijah Hawkins—this man Joseph was so afraid of—and then I wanted to tell him to go to hell.

"Please, Dee. He can't know you're awake yet or he'll want to take over."

Joseph grabbed the knife off the table and bent down in front of me. He looked at my arm before sliding one of the metal bowls forward. I tensed up, terrified that he was calculating which part of my arm to slice into next.

"Don't," I begged. I would've said anything, done anything he asked right then if he'd just let me go.

"I'm not doing this to hurt you. I'm doing this to keep you safe."

Hurt me? He wasn't going to *hurt* me? What kind of idiot did he take me for? The crisscross pattern of marks lining my arms were his doing. The metal pans filled with my blood were his doing. And the blade he held to my forearm was certainly all him.

"Close your eyes, Dee," he said again, and I did everything in my power to open them wider, to stare at him with what little defiance and courage I could gather. If he was going to do this, then I wasn't going to make it easy for him. He was going to have to look me in the eyes as he sliced me up.

I caught the slight tremor in his hand as he pushed the blade in. The pain didn't bother me. It stung but nothing more. I could even handle the blackish red seeping from my arm. What did me in was the sound of my blood hitting the metal pan.

My world spun. The only thing anchoring me to the present was the earth-shattering sound of the dripping. I could hear Joseph speaking. It was as if he were calling me from the end of a tunnel, his voice warped and drawn out as he told me to let go.

I did as he said. I let go of everything and welcomed the darkness hovering around the edges of my mind.

FIFTEEN

I'd been moved. The soft quilt tucked around me and the smell of hot food told me that much. A quick scan of the room confirmed my suspicions. The cinderblock walls were gone, beige plaster boxing me in. Two plain beds without headboards sat side by side, and I was lying in one. The other was neatly made, with a white-and-gold quilt covering the sheets. There was a nightstand, two wooden chairs, and a pine dresser with some sort of big glass bowl sitting on top of it. Above me was a clock and a window. Full-sized. No bars. Just a plain old wooden window covered with lace curtains.

Slowly, I sat up, my eyes immediately trailing down my arms. Bandages covered my forearms from wrist to elbow. I pressed down on one gently, wincing as pain shot through me. The throbbing in my head had given way to a dull ache. It hurt, but at least I could think past it. Reaching up to the back of my head, I swept my hair aside and uncovered yet another bandage and an extremely tender section of scalp.

My mind raced back to the basement, to Joseph's whispers, to the footsteps and the pinch in my arm that had sent my entire world reeling into darkness. I struggled through the haze, trying to remember how I got here, who'd carried me, and what route they took. But it was all a blur. One horrific, migraine-inducing blur.

I scooted back, pulling the quilt with me. A quick peek under the blankets let me know I was completely dressed. It didn't mean anything, not when I'd been unconscious for God knows how long. But for some reason, that extra layer of cotton made me feel safer.

The door eased open and Joseph walked in, eying the bed before taking a seat across the room.

"Where am I?" I asked.

"In our reintegration facilities."

I stared at him, trying to wrap my head around that word. *Reintegration.*

He laughed, a familiar sound that did little to relax me. "Stop thinking so hard. It's nothing more than a fancy name for the rooms behind the chapel."

I gazed back at the window, honing in on the small metal bracket on the top of the frame. It was a standard latch, one that locked from the inside. I glanced at the door. No visible lock there at all. Nothing. Absolutely nothing preventing me from bolting.

As easy as it appeared, I doubted it'd be that simple.

Joseph saw my wandering eyes and guessed what I was thinking. "It's not the locks you need to be worried about."

I ignored his warning and got up to test my balance, half expecting to topple over from the blood loss. I didn't, which meant I'd probably been out of it longer than I wanted to know.

I moved toward the door, and Joseph placed himself squarely between me and my escape route. "What I meant was that the door isn't locked, but it would be a bad idea to try to walk out. Believe me, you won't get more than five feet down that hall before he sees you."

I looked up. No cameras, no blinking red lights, and no strange men peering in the window. Which meant whoever *he* was, he was waiting outside that door. S'okay, I'd deal with him too.

"Mm hmm," I said as I did a quick sweep of the room for my shoes and socks. My bare feet were freezing, and if I had a prayer of escaping, I'd need them.

Joseph's hand was on my shoulder in an instant, his eyes dark. Troubled. He pulled back quickly, like a man who'd touched a hot coal. "I'm serious. The only reason you're conscious now is because I agreed to stay here and keep watch over you. He would've made me keep bleeding you if he'd had his way. I'm supposed to keep you from walking into the chapel or making contact with anyone else until I've had a chance to explain things to you. Until he can see for himself that you understand your new role here." He maneuvered me back toward the bed. "Please, Dee, sit back down."

I tried to yank myself free from his grip, but Joseph was

every bit as strong as he looked. Maybe stronger. "So you're the only reason I'm conscious?" I yelled. "That's ironic, considering you're the one that bled me in the first place!" I stumbled backward as he released his hold, then snatched my shoes and socks from beneath the bed and jammed my feet into them. "And explain what to me?"

"I don't know ... *things*. And I didn't want it to be this way," Joseph whispered, his attention darting nervously between me and the door. "There wasn't a choice."

"Who are you trying to kid? You had a dozen other choices. Dozens! And you made the wrong one."

"I made the only choice that would save my sister."

"Whatever," I said, completely uninterested in debating the morality of kidnapping. "Where are Luke and Mike?" I hoped they were in the next town by now, telling the police all about the Purity Springs and their community of deranged freaks.

Joseph's voice was so low, so quiet I had to strain to make out his words. "I already told you, they're not here."

I racked my brain for any bit of useless information, anything that might help me get out or make contact with Luke. I knew what to do if the man with razors on his hands attacked me in my dreams. I could tell you which way to run if an awkward kid rose from the lake, fully grown and wearing a hockey mask. I was even prepared to get off the damn plane when seven random kids from some stupid French class went nuts over the fear of it crashing. But I had no idea what to do when faced with a self-proclaimed prophet and his entire batshit town.

The sound of a door opening and closing outside my room interrupted my thoughts, and Joseph shoved me toward the bed. "Take your shoes off and get back into bed," he hissed. "Now!"

I half-debated staying right there to meet his father, but I didn't get a chance. Joseph shoved me again, harder this time, and I fell onto the bed. I fought him as he went to pull the quilt over me. Eventually he gave up and left me there, my shoes hanging off my feet, my legs tangled in the quilt.

SIXTEEN

The door swung open and a middle-aged man walked in. He was holding a tray of food and an oversized manila envelope. With a head of graying hair, glasses, and deep smile lines around his eyes, he looked like half the dads I'd seen at school. Just as benign, too.

He closed the door quickly, pausing until Joseph took a step forward and bowed his head.

"Father," Joseph said, his voice hushed.

I took a long look at Elijah Hawkins, then shook my head. This was the man Joseph had warned me about? The man who had abused children and murdered his own wife? It wasn't possible. This guy looked like he was more likely to pack some lures and go fly-fishing than he was to lead a deadly cult.

"Have a seat, son," Elijah said, his voice deeper, louder than I expected. Setting the tray on the nightstand, he turned his gaze on me.

He was studying me, his eyes lingering on my face before traveling downward. They stopped at my chest, then continued on to my waist and down my legs. In my panic, I'd only pulled the quilt halfway up my body, leaving my entire left leg uncovered, my shoelaces untied and dangling.

"Going somewhere?" he asked, pointing at my foot.

I stayed silent, refusing to acknowledge him. I wasn't going to let this aging man wearing a plaid button-up shirt intimidate me. He was half the size of Luke and three times his age. No way could he be as strong or fast. Even with my arms bandaged and a vicious knot on my head, I could probably take him.

"No sir, she wasn't going anywhere," Joseph answered for me. "I bled her for quite a while, so she's still a little woozy. Plus, she's too weak to make it far."

Joseph was talking fast, too fast, and Elijah held up a hand for him to stop. "I asked *her*, Joseph, not you." His steely eyes focused on me again, lingering on my legs. I wished I'd opted for something a bit more unflattering than skinny jeans. Perhaps snow pants or a mangy pair of sweats.

"What do you want from me?" I asked.

Elijah inhaled loudly. "You know my wife died," he started, and I nodded. "Joseph was understandably upset. No doubt felt as betrayed as I did."

"Betrayed?" I asked. I'd gotten that emotion from Joseph, but Elijah? He was the one who'd killed her.

"Yes, betrayed. About my wife having to die, that is. I've given my life to this town, ensuring that the people under my care remain pure as I lead them in God's path," Elijah explained. "It's been my duty, as it was my father's and his father's before that. We have kept this town innocent, safe from outside influences, for over a hundred and fifty years. Someday, that responsibility will be Joseph's."

Not if Joseph had his way. From what he'd told me, he was only hanging around here long enough to grab his sister, then he was gone.

"I have guided this town for nearly eighteen years, watched as we, as a community, have grown closer to God," Elijah continued. "Never once did I complain or question *His* mission for me. So when I, a prophet who has selflessly given my life to the Lord's work, was asked to sacrifice my own wife for the greater good, yes, I admit I felt betrayed."

Elijah smiled dryly, as if reliving a bittersweet memory. "Joseph is my son. My only son." He sat down next to me on the bed and reached out to touch my calf. I went to pull away and he clamped his hand down on my ankle, holding me in place.

I sat as still as I possibly could and tried to ignore the bile rising in my throat. The old man's gaze followed the stroking path his fingers were making on my calf, and my heart hammered against my chest as his fingers slid upward. I glanced at Joseph, but he made no move to help.

"I understand now, though. *His* plan all along was for me to lose my blessed wife so I could gain you. See, I need more children, more Hawkins sons to carry on our family's legacy. And you, my dear, are going to give them to me."

Elijah's words plowed through my brain with all the intensity of a raging fire. I didn't know whether to laugh or scream at him. The complete sincerity in his voice made absolutely no sense.

I stopped his hand short of my thigh and dug my nails into his palm. "Children? You actually think God gave me to you? You think I'm actually going to sleep with you? Have you lost your—"

Joseph jumped up from his seat, the wooden chair he was sitting on crashing to the floor. His movements were forced, deliberate, like he'd stood up and purposefully kicked the chair over to get his father's attention. Didn't matter; it worked, and Elijah pulled his hand back, refocusing his glare on his son.

"What has Joseph told you?" Elijah asked.

I took a quick look at Joseph before I lied. "Nothing."

Elijah's grin faded, leaving behind a cold expression. "I asked you to speak with her, Joseph." There was a ring of disapproval there, one that promised retribution. "I expected her to be prepared, to have at least some knowledge of her place here."

"I spoke with her," Joseph replied, and I racked my brain for any hint of that conversation. As hard as I tried, I got nothing. Joseph was lying.

"But as I said," Joseph continued, his eyes pleading with me to play along. "I purified her like you asked. She was confused when she finally came to; I think I bled her more thoroughly then I should have. I told her how important she was to us, but I don't think she remembers any of it. Now that she is more alert, perhaps you can explain it to her."

Elijah nodded, and for a second I let myself believe he'd bought Joseph's excuse.

"I know it makes no sense to you now, but in time you'll see the wisdom of what I say." Elijah handed me the envelope, his fingers twisting the edge of the thick yellow paper as he spoke. "In time, you too will be made pure."

"What's this?" I asked

"This is you. Your new life. Past and present," Elijah re-plied.

He leaned back on the bed, a deep smile spreading across his face. I wanted to spit at him, to tell him that he was a psycho and that my life wasn't going to include him or his crazy family. But I didn't say any of that. Rather, I slid a finger beneath the flap of the envelope and pulled out the papers.

Rebekah Hawkins, wife of Elijah Hawkins.
Seventeen years of age. Born in Purity Springs.
Baptized into the Church of the Divine Light.
Educated by the sole hand of Elijah Hawkins,
secluded to preserve her purity.

"I don't get it," I said, confused as to what any of this crap had to do with me.

"Keep reading," Elijah said, nudging the papers in my hand.

Birth parents—Samuel and Abilene Smith.
Sacrificed and martyred in the name of the Church.
Brought forth as the divine wife of Elijah Hawkins this day,
November 8th, the year of the Great Lord.

I stopped reading and flicked my wrist to see my watch. Today was the eighth. The ninth was Sunday, the day the Hoopers were expecting me home.

"Still not getting it," I said again. "Why do I care about Rebekah Hawkins?"

Elijah tapped the paper and then lifted my chin to meet his eyes. "Because as of today, *you* are Rebekah Hawkins."

SEVENTEEN

I yanked my chin out of Elijah's grip, desperate to get away from him. His words held the promise of something more. The kind of something I wanted no part of.

The papers fell from my hands and floated to the floor. The same trapped, helpless feeling I'd felt for so many years washed over me. I kept waiting for Joseph to do or say something... anything. He didn't. He sat there with his gaze fixed on me in that same silent warning. The one that told me to keep my mouth shut and do as his father said.

I went to get off the bed, but Elijah shifted with me, his body shadowing mine. He was close, so close. I told myself that if I could get my legs loose from the quilt, then I could kick him.

I tore the quilt from my body and threw myself at Elijah, intent on clawing my way through him to get to the door. He caught me mid-strike, his hands banding around my upper arms. His breath was ragged, his grip growing tighter as he tried to hold my jerking body still.

I saw Joseph out of the corner of my eye and tried to squeeze out the word "please." Joseph's eyes widened, and a low hiss of breath escaped his lips. But he didn't move. He wasn't going to help me. All he wanted was to get his sister out, and he didn't care who he screwed over in the process.

Elijah loosened his hold and blood rushed back into my tingling hands. When I didn't come at him again, he let me go completely.

"I understand that you're confused and a bit scared about the path God has chosen for you. But I assure you that you are not alone. I am here to guide you, to teach you," he said as he bent over to pick up the papers scattered across the floor. "It is time for you to listen, *Rebekah*. You're going to read every word written here. You're going to memorize them, because it is the only way to rid you of your past, of the life that has tainted you. This is your history now. Your rebirth. This is you."

Screw self-preservation. I had to know. "And if I don't?"

He laughed, a maniacal sound that had me wishing I'd kept my mouth shut. "You've seen too much of the outside world, my sweet girl. But have no fear, it only means I need to be overly sure that you are cleansed of the evil you were once immersed in. In time, you will come to rely upon my wisdom, understand my responsibilities, and accept my divine authority."

I shook my head; he hadn't answered my question. "And. If. I. Don't?"

Elijah tossed out his hands, amused by my persistence. "You'll find me to be peaceful man. We are a peaceful town. But as Joseph can tell you, I find that fear and pain work equally as well as reason. In a matter of days, you will come to see the truth of my words and embrace your new life, your salvation. If not...well, I'd hate for us to start our life together under those circumstances. And make no mistake about it, Rebekah. You now belong to me."

"I won't stay," I said, unsure of where that flash of courage came from. "You can't keep me. I have a family that will come looking for me. Friends." *And Luke*, I silently added.

I wasn't sure if the Hoopers counted as family, but I had a place to live, and people who liked having me around. I was almost a full person again, and I'd be damned if this man was going to take it away from me now.

"Yes, friends. All right, we can play it that way. Joseph?" Elijah called, and Joseph took two steps toward his father as if he were a puppet and Elijah controlled his strings.

"I'm not sure if my son has told you, but he has a younger sister," Elijah said.

"Eden," I whispered.

"Yes, Eden," Elijah replied. "Joseph is quite fond of his sister. He takes on more responsibility for her than he should. He sees himself as her protector. My guess is he'll do the same for you."

I had no clue what Elijah was getting at. I knew Joseph

was hell-bent on getting his sister out, but he'd done absolutely nothing to help me. In fact, he'd done everything he could to trap me here, including slicing me open.

"One of Joseph's greatest strengths, what will make him such a great leader, is that he is a good judge of character," Elijah said. "I'm presuming he's figured out you have a soft side, one he's depending on you to help him with Eden."

Joseph clenched his hands at his side, his gaze remaining steady and cool despite the revelation that Elijah apparently knew about his plotting. I stared at Joseph as he stood unblinking and still as a statue, wondering what he was thinking. Was he afraid? Pissed? I had no clue, but I had to hold on to the hope that the one thing he wasn't was resigned.

Elijah smiled, then turned his attention from Joseph to me. "If you give me any problem, if you so much as question your newfound role in Purity Springs, then I'm going to beat my son here to within an inch of his life. The pain will be so bad he'll wish he were dead. But I won't give him the mercy of death, not until he tells me where he's stashed those two boys you're with. And as for them … I'll rid them from this earth rather than risk contaminating my town with their filth. Do you understand?"

My breath caught in my throat as the truth bore into me. Elijah's knowledge wasn't restricted to Joseph's plan to free Eden … he knew about Luke and Mike as well. He'd been aware of us from the very beginning.

"I will remind you once more not to test me." Elijah leaned in so that his breath whispered across mine as he spoke. "I assure you that you will not win. In the end, you'll be sitting in exactly the same position as you are now, bound to me and this town. I'll kill your two friends, Joseph too if I have to. But not you. You, I have plans for."

He pulled back and handed me the papers. "If you don't believe me, ask Joseph. He will be happy to remind you exactly who I am and the respect I command. He's got the scars to prove it."

I glanced at Joseph. He was standing there silent, his lips pressed into a thin, tight line. No wonder he seemed to get me. He was living my life. My old life. If I hadn't been so scared, I would've laughed at the irony. Here I was, away on a weekend where I was supposed to be celebrating my anniversary with Luke, and instead I was trapped in a hellhole with a delusional man, at the mercy of his equally damaged son.

Elijah took my stunned silence as assent and ran his hand down the side of my face, lingering on my cheek before tucking a stray piece of hair behind my ear. I'd think the gesture fatherly, almost soothing, had it not been for the crazy shit he'd just unloaded on me.

"Now that we have that settled, *Rebekah*, let's get you cleaned up and introduced to your new family." He walked over to the dresser and sifted through the top drawer, taking a few items out. He held them up, judging them for size, then swapped them for a smaller, matching set.

They were plain, nothing more than a long all-white skirt and a shirt that covered everything from wrist to chin. Clean and neatly folded, there was not a single color to be found.

Elijah dropped them onto the bed and pulled a bottle from his pocket. "The polish needs to come off your nails," he said as he placed the nail polish remover on the dresser. "Your makeup is pretty much worn off, but you should give your face a good scrub anyway. Then fix your hair. Nothing fancy. A plain braid down the middle will do fine."

I watched as he assembled all the necessary items—a bar of soap, a black hair tie, a scratchy white towel not big enough to cover much of anything, and a pair of beige clogs.

"That basin there is filled with water," Elijah said, gesturing to the glass bowl on the dresser. "Give the clothes you are wearing, undergarments included, to Joseph. He'll burn them along with any trace of your former life. This is a new beginning for you, Rebekah, your chance at a better life. I can guarantee you an eternity of peace and happiness. Embrace your new self. Embrace me."

I nodded and forced a smile to my face. I wasn't consenting to anything, and I had no intention of relinquishing my jeans and bra to anyone. But I wanted him out of the room, and agreeing to wash up and change seemed like the quickest way to do that. Once he was gone, I was going to get out of here. Clothes, nail polish, underwear and all.

"And once I'm changed?" I asked, trying to figure out how much time I had.

"I will introduce you to your new family, to my followers. They are excited to meet you."

"I bet they are," I mumbled under my breath.

Joseph brought a finger up to his lips, warning me to stay quiet. Too late. Elijah heard me and was already turning around.

"You say something?" he asked.

I doubted he wanted an answer. It seemed more like a challenge than anything else, but I responded nonetheless. "No, not a thing."

"Good. I'll leave these with you," he said, gesturing to the documents outlining my fictional past. "I think you will find it quite thorough, but if you have any questions, you ask me. *Only* me. Is that understood?"

"Yes."

"Good. Joseph will stay here with you while you prepare. We had a bit of a chat after he brought you to me this morning, didn't we, son?" Elijah turned to Joseph, who nodded. "I'm quite sure he no longer needs to be reminded of his duties within the community."

I looked at Joseph, wondering what Elijah was talking about, why his use of the word "chat" made me nauseated.

"And welcome home, Rebekah."

EIGHTEEN

I crept over to the door and listened, holding my tongue until his footsteps faded away. Then I let loose on Joseph

I wanted answers. I wouldn't let up until I knew where he was holding Luke and Mike. I wanted to know when Elijah ate. When he slept. When he went to the bathroom. I needed to know every last detail of his schedule so I could sneak away without him noticing.

"Where are they?" I hissed, my body vibrating with a lethal mix of fear and rage. "Tell me right now where Luke and Mike are or so help me God I'll—"

I went to smack Joseph, to punch him, to do whatever it would take to drag the truth out of him, but he caught me, trapping my wrists against his chest with his hands. "Dee, don't," he whispered softly. "You can get angry with me all you want, but I'd lose that tone before you speak to my father again."

Joseph was in no position to give me advice; it was his fault I was here in the first place. And I'd speak to his father any way I pleased. "Are you out of your mind?" I screamed. "Who gave you the—"

He held up a hand for me to stop. Instinctively, I shut up and looked at the door. It was closed; no jingling knob, no footsteps, and no muffled voices on the other side.

I slowed my breathing and refocused on my goal rather than my building rage. "Where is Luke? What did you do to him?" I asked again.

"Why can't you trust me on this? I told you, they're fine."

"Trust you? Are you kidding me?"

I picked up the pile of clothes his father had left for me and threw them at Joseph. "You kidnapped me, drained half my blood, and then bartered me away as your father's bride in some sick attempt to save your sister. I don't know about you, but where I come from, that doesn't breed trust. Now where are Luke and Mike?"

"They're locked in the shed," he quickly said, his mind obviously on something else. "And what do you mean, 'bartered you away' to my father?"

"In the shed. The one we were hiding out in? The Livor?" I asked, running through the layout of that dark, ten-by-ten-foot structure in my head. I looked up at the clock on the wall. It was one in the afternoon. If I was calculating right, then they'd been there five, maybe six hours tops. Not enough time to starve or become dehydrated, but plenty of time to lose their minds. I hadn't thought to check the thickness of the walls, but Luke was strong, and Mike had one set of lungs and a nasty temper to go with it.

What little hope I'd managed to hang onto faded the instant Joseph started talking. "I turned the irrigation pump on before I left. Nobody will hear them over that noise. And believe me, that's a good thing. You don't want them found by anyone around here anyway."

I shrugged off his words. Luke was used to tackling two-hundred-pound kids on the football field. Mike too. That old shed with its scratched-up walls was no match for them.

"And where did you get the idea that I'd give you to my father in exchange for my sister?" Joseph asked, repeating his original question. He looked confused, maybe even a bit offended.

I turned away from him, annoyed. If he was too stupid to figure that one out, then I wasn't going to help. "Nothing. Forget it."

"I meant what I said earlier, Dee."

"Isn't it *Rebekah* now? And you said a lot of things, most of them lies," I fired back.

"I never lied to you," he yelled.

I laughed. I couldn't help it—his profession of innocence was so damn absurd it was funny.

"I. Didn't." He took a step closer and stared down at me. I swallowed hard and stepped back, kept right on going until my knees hit the mattress, forcing me to sit down.

Joseph saw the flicker of panic cross my face and backed up. "I promise I won't hurt you, *Dee*," he said placing extra emphasis on my name. "But please, slow down and listen to me for a minute."

He unbuttoned his shirt, deliberately keeping his attention on me as the white of his undershirt came into view. There was a slowness to his movements and a barely audible wince of pain under his breath. I scooted farther away from him, confused. I had no clue what was going on, but the more-than-obvious pain on Joseph's face told me one thing for sure. Joseph wasn't planning on hurting me, not in that way anyway.

"You think you've had a tough time here? That my father has treated you badly? You haven't seen half of what he can do," Joseph warned.

He turned around and lifted his undershirt up over his head. The fabric caught in spots, the thin white cotton adhering itself to the weeping wounds. Red welts marked his back, each one strategically placed to hit more flesh than bone. I knew exactly what they were, my mind flashing back to the black leather belt my father was so fond of wearing. There'd been no "chat" that morning, no peaceful reminder to fall back in line. Elijah had beaten him with a belt.

My dad only hit me with a belt once, and it was a long time ago. But I remembered it well, still cringed whenever Luke took his belt off. Joseph might hurt now, but if memory served me right, those marks would sting like hell the second day, when the slightest of movements would force them to crack and re-open.

"He did that to you?" I asked.

It wasn't a question, but Joseph nodded anyway.

"He tried to get you to tell him where they are, didn't he?" I asked, and Joseph shrugged. "Why didn't you tell him? Why would you let him do that to you in order to protect Luke and Mike?"

I couldn't wrap my brain around any of this. We'd downright refused to come in here willingly and save his sister. Yet Joseph had taken a beating to protect them, to protect me. That made absolutely no sense.

"I was raised in this. I've been hit more times than you can imagine. Don't worry," he said with a weak smile. "I won't break. If he starts in on me again about where they are, I won't give into the pain. I figured you would, so . . ."

No, I wouldn't. I hadn't yet. I didn't break during the thirteen years I lived with my father, or when the girls in the group home taught me my place. And I definitely wasn't planning on breaking now.

But Joseph had no way of knowing that.

"I know what you must think of me. But try to remember, I never had a choice in any of this. Nothing here is as black and white as it seems, Dee. You can't simply decide you want to leave one day and get up and go. It doesn't work that way."

"That's not true," I argued.

"You're an idiot if you think that," Joseph replied. "My mom and I planned our escape for over a year. We hid all of our tracks, and he *still* found out. If you want to get out of here, then we have to play his game for now. Let him think he's won, buy me some time to figure something out . . . a way that gets all of us away from him."

When he said "all," he didn't just mean us and Luke and Mike. He meant Eden too. That would take time, and time was the one thing I didn't have. "How long do I have to play along?" I asked.

Joseph ran a hand through his hair and sighed. "Luke was pretty clear about not helping me save my sister, but I'd stake my life on the fact that he'll come in here to get you."

"And?"

"Well, I'm banking on that—not only for Eden's life and mine, but for yours too."

I shook my head. If that was his plan—waiting on Luke to come to me—then he was dumber than I thought. I had no intention of sitting around here, dressing up and playing Elijah's bride. I was outta here, with or without Joseph and his precious Eden.

But for the first time since I'd met Joseph, it felt like I had leverage, something I could use to force his hand. Luke.

NINETEEN

"Let's go get them now," I said. Luke could help; he *would* help. "If it makes you feel better, I promise we'll come back for Eden. You have my word."

"We can't. Not yet. We need to give my father some time to let his guard down."

"How long?" I asked again. In my mind, right now was the perfect time. I couldn't shake the vision of Luke and Mike locked in that shed, screaming with no one around to hear them. Freezing as the temperature dropped with nightfall, huddled into each other, hungry and tired but unwilling to sleep. The image was terrifying, but like staring at the wreckage of a deadly crash, I couldn't seem to pull away.

"Dee," Joseph said, shaking me. I hadn't realized he was trying to get my attention. I was too lost in my living nightmare to even hear him speak.

I looked up and met his stare, pleading with him to take my side and go get them now. "They don't have any food or water. It's freezing out. They'll—"

"No they won't," Joseph interrupted. "I've survived out there a lot longer."

He took my hand and led me over to the chair, then picked up the papers outlining my new life and laid them on the dresser for me to see.

I stared down at the papers, the words blurring into one giant black spot. I went to say something, to argue my case for leaving right now, when he put his fingers to my lips, stopping me.

"Trust me, Dee, please. Play along for a little while. Like I said, once he lets his guard down, we can take Eden and slip out."

Somewhere in this messed-up conversation, I'd come to the terrifying conclusion that I might have to give up control. Maybe Joseph was right—sometimes you had to place your faith in the untrustworthy to survive.

"What do you want me to do?" I asked.

"Memorize this," he said. "If you don't, none of us have a chance."

I glanced at the papers, scanning for the information that seemed to be the most important. If I'd had a month, maybe I could've memorized it all. But less than a few hours wasn't nearly enough time.

Joseph handed me the clothes Elijah had set out. I took them and exhaled. I got why he couldn't leave his sister behind, understood more than he probably realized. And I wasn't saying that I didn't want to help. I just wasn't sure I could.

"Can I ask you some questions?" I asked, and he nodded. "Why is your father keeping such close tabs on Eden? He pretty much said that it was you who would eventually lead this town, so why does he care so much about her?"

"She's important to my father. Valuable. She's the only daughter of our . . ." He paused only long enough to correct himself. "The only daughter of this town's prophet. The first girl to be born to the Hawkins family in over three generations."

I shook my head, not understanding what he was getting at. I was my father's only daughter. Hell, I was his only child, and that didn't seem to make a difference to him or his fists.

"My father protects her, spares her from the disciplinary actions most of us receive. He wants to keep her thoughts as pure as her body. Eden has no reason to be afraid of him, no reason to think about leaving."

I felt like I'd been punched in the gut. Joseph was putting both our lives on the line for his sister, and she didn't want to leave. "So let me get this straight. You dragged me in here, risking not only my life but Luke's and Mike's, and your sister wants to *stay?*"

His face fell. Joseph knew what he was doing, what he was asking of me, and for once I was glad to see a flash of shame. "You don't understand, Dee. She's young, barely twelve. She has no idea what he has planned for her or the discipline a husband is expected to exact on his wife. My mother hid it from her. He'll marry her off in less than two years as a way to secure the most influential of his followers to him. She won't survive it. She can't."

I thought back to when I was twelve and remembered how hard it was to find the strength to get up and leave everything behind. It took me an entire year to do it, to finally admit to a judge what my father had done to me and ask to be taken away from him for good. Those were things no child should ever have to do, and yet I had.

Joseph handed me the skirt Elijah had laid out and motioned for me to get up. "You need to get dressed and start reading."

I slipped my shoes from my feet and waited for Joseph to head for the door. He caught my look and turned his back, but didn't leave.

"Can I get a little privacy?" I asked.

"Nope. I'm staying. You're safer with me in here," he argued. "Now go on and change."

My cheeks flushed as I undid the button of my jeans and hastily stripped them off. Tossing my shirt aside, I grasped the cotton shirt and yanked it down over my head then pulled on the skirt.

"You can turn around now," I said as I twisted my hair into an ugly braid. "And I have more questions for you."

"I figured you would. Go ahead," he said.

"These people who are supposed to be my parents— Samuel and Abeline Smith—who are they?"

Joseph shrugged. "I have no idea. There was a couple who died in a house fire about ten years back. Their last name was Smith, but I think the husband's name was Nathaniel or something. And I don't think they had any children, but then again, my father could've fabricated the whole thing. Knowing him, they never existed."

"This doesn't make any sense," I muttered. "He makes up entire families? How is that even possible? How has he never been found out?"

"What's to find out?" Joseph asked as he handed me the pair of clogs I was expected to wear.

I grabbed the clogs from his hand and jammed my feet into them. "Oh, I don't know, kidnapping? Maybe child abuse? Neglect? Murder? Take your pick."

"And who would report it?" he asked, unfazed.

His question was so honest, yet so unfathomable. "So you're saying that no one here, not one person in God knows how many years, ever realized that your father is nuts? That what he's doing is wrong?"

"I never said that, but you've got to go some distance to find a town that he doesn't control."

"What does that even mean?" I snapped. Joseph's tone was serious, but I didn't have the time or the patience to play twenty questions. I thought back to the last town we'd passed, the one with an abundance of Twinkies and the gas station we *didn't* use. They'd seemed normal, friendly.

"I've been told that my Grandfather wasn't as strict of a leader as my father, that for generations several of the men were allowed to work outside of Purity Springs. All their money went into Purity Springs' communal pool, but they worked in neighboring towns, nonetheless."

I nodded; that would explain how the town survived,

financially anyway. "What changed? Why aren't people allowed to leave anymore?"

"My father happened. When he took over, he called them all back. He said the risk of being exposed to the true evils of the world was too great, and that he needed them close by, where he could protect them."

"So that was what, like, seventeen years ago? A lot can change in seventeen years."

"Not in those towns," Joseph continued, his attention flicking toward the window. "He left two people outside, two people he could trust. His brothers. One is the sheriff in a town about fifty miles north of here called Camden Hills. The other sits on the town council of a tiny farming community to the east. Other than those two towns, there's no one around here to even notice us."

That made absolutely no sense. Surely anybody who had the chance to live outside this place would never come back, never mind help Elijah. "I get that they're his brothers and all, but in their jobs, they must interact with people from outside this town all the time. They know we're not all evil."

"They grew up here," Joseph said matter-of-factly.

What? Was he drinking his own Kool-Aid? You couldn't tell me that being born and raised here meant you couldn't see the truth. Couldn't see the real Elijah. His mom had, and if what Joseph was saying was true, then he had as well.

I threw my hands out, dismissing his answer. "Not buying it."

"Their families live here, Dee. My aunts ... my cousins all live here in Purity Springs."

I tried to wrap my brain around this, around the notion of two men, intelligent enough to hold decent jobs, leaving their families behind in this town with a madman. I couldn't.

"Do *they* want to leave?" I asked, wondering if their wives were part of the group Joseph's mom had planned to come back for. "The families?"

"No."

His answer left little room for reply, so I let it go and moved on to something more pressing. "So why not go farther, skip those two towns and keep going?"

He didn't answer immediately, just studied me for a minute as if judging the validity of my question. "Come here," he said and held out his hand.

I followed him over to the window above the bed. He leaned over and pulled the curtains back, gesturing for me to have a look. "Do any of them look abused to you? Unhealthy? Miserable? From the outside, there's nothing to report."

I peered out the window, squinting against the midday sun. The street was littered with people, and he was right—not a single one looked beaten down or broken. They looked . . . content.

Across the street was the bank. An older man was hanging up a *closed* sign while another was on a ladder, changing what appeared to be the bulb in a streetlight. A young girl, probably no older than seven, was sweeping the front steps of the tiny diner, smiling at Elijah as he walked past. Then a car passed by, pulled into the gas station, and actually *got* gas.

"When?" I pressed my face to the glass, wondering when this town had gone from completely abandoned to fully operational. "When did all of this happen? When did they all come back out?"

"About ten minutes after I brought you in."

Joseph must've seen the confused look cross my face, because he eased me down onto the bed and waited for my breathing to slow before he continued. "The alarms that were going off when you came into town—I pulled them."

I nodded. He'd already told me that.

"They're our way of alerting people of an emergency. No different from what other small towns have, I suppose."

"Um hmm," I mumbled, not bothering to tell him that normal people, people who took advantage of things like phones and TVs, had something called the emergency broadcast system and Weather Bug, but whatever.

"We have one police officer and a volunteer fire department. They all live here. They were all born and raised *here*. We use the sirens to alert them when they're needed. Works if there's a bad storm coming or if my father needs to gather his people."

"Can they hear it in the neighboring towns?" I asked, hoping that somebody with no blood ties to Purity Springs would get curious and come looking.

"No, but it doesn't matter. If my father needs them, his brothers will come."

"And?" I said, waving my hands to hurry him along.

"When the sirens go off, everyone gathers in the chapel. It didn't take my father long to figure out I was missing and that I pulled the alarm. He held everybody there until he could figure out what I was up to."

"The car," I muttered.

"Yeah, that's when he found your car. But once he decided the town was safe, after I brought you in, things went back to normal."

"And they believe him," I said, gesturing toward the window. "They actually believe the crap he feeds them?"

"Yes."

It was one word. Complete and absolute. Brooking no challenge.

I thought of this town, of the one hundred and forty-eight residents worshiping Elijah, and I groaned. "Oh my God. Here I was thinking all along that the only person we needed to beat was your dad. But there's a whole town out there. Every single one of them thinks I belong to them, that I was born and raised for them!"

"And two towns beyond that," he added, reminding me how far his father's hold extended. "It's possible, though. I don't know exactly how yet, but it's possible to get out of here. It's happened before, and it can happen again."

TWENTY

His words caught my attention, and I looked up. "Who? When?"

That fact that somebody had managed to escape Elijah Hawkins's hold was exactly what I needed to hear. Then it hit me. "Mary."

Joseph grinned, one of the first genuine smiles I'd seen from him. "Yes, my Aunt Mary. My mother's sister."

"Where is she now? How did she do it?"

"I don't know exactly. My mother never talked about it, and it wasn't my place to ask. But I think something happened, something involving my father."

I didn't bother to press for details. I'd spent less than an hour with Elijah Hawkins and that was plenty enough time for my mind to fill in the blanks. And none of those blanks were good.

"She got up in the middle of the night and took off. She knew my uncles controlled the surrounding towns. Everybody does. She drove over three hundred miles until she finally stopped and told the police about Purity Springs, about my father..."

"And?" I prompted. I didn't have time for him to get lost in thought. I wanted information. I wanted to know the exact route his aunt had taken, how she'd managed to slip away undetected, and whether Elijah had ever caught up with her.

"The police took her statement, and they *did* come looking. She brought two officers back with her, along with a woman who claimed to work for the some social services agency. They were here for two days. They questioned nearly everyone, including my mother, but found nothing."

"How is that possible?" I asked, remembering the books we'd found. They were like ledgers, cataloging what punishments were doled out and when. You couldn't get better proof than that.

"Think about it, Dee. Does my dad look strange to you? Does Purity Springs look at all off?"

I considered his question for half a second, then realized he was right. Sure, the houses were a little outdated, and the town had a weird vibe to it, but they drank milk with dinner. They sold Pringles at the gas station. They had streetlights and a bank. To the outside world, yeah... they looked normal.

"What about the books and shed with all the claw marks? That room you were—" I stopped as the words caught in my throat and the memories came rushing back. The plinking sound. The blood dripping from my arms into the small silver bowl. "The room you bled me in."

"The isolation room can easily pass as an irrigation shed. Every farming community has one. And *that* room … well, that's part of an unfinished basement. The floor is tiled for obvious reasons, but to anyone else, it looks like nothing more than a cellar."

"But what about the kids? I saw the books, Joseph. I know what their parents do to them."

"Punishment is a form of guidance. Of love. The adults don't see it as wrong. As for the kids, well, two things. They fear my father's retribution, and that fear keeps them from telling the truth. Plus, my father isn't stupid; he always takes the mental route first. He only resorts to physical violence when he can't get through to them any other way. And trust me, sometimes you'd rather be hit than deal with the stuff he can unload on you."

Joseph stopped speaking and refocused his gaze on the window, then back at me. "That and the fact that the worst of it was always reserved for me."

"What happened to your aunt?" I asked. He hadn't answered my question or given me the details I needed.

"We've got our own police, you know. Our own school. Own doctor. Own coroner. We pay our taxes like everybody else and have virtually no crime. There's nothing in the records that my father doesn't want to be there."

I swallowed hard as a familiar pang of hopelessness burrowed its way into me like a disease. He was ignoring my question again, talking about things that wouldn't help me escape. "Answer me, Joseph. What happened to your Aunt Mary?"

"The authorities found nothing to back up her claims. All they saw were happy, well-adjusted children and loving families. However, they did find an entire file on my Aunt Mary showing years of delusional behavior complete with medication logs and a brief stint at a privately run, extremely exclusive psychiatric hospital."

I clenched my hands, desperately trying to make sense of what he was saying. "What? Are you telling me she was crazy?"

Joseph crouched down in front of me, bringing himself to eye-level. "No, Dee. She was one of the sanest people I knew. But she did everything wrong. You can't spout off to my father and threaten to leave. Because, like he did for you, he created a whole new identity for her. One that served *his* needs."

"But she got out!" I yelled, clinging to the hope that we could too.

"Maybe, but nobody on the outside will ever believe a word she says about him or this town. He made sure of that."

"He can label me crazy all he wants, but I won't stay here."

"*We* won't stay," he corrected me. "But I need you to play along and let him think he has the upper hand, at least until I can convince Eden to run."

"So I need to be Rebekah," I whispered, locking my gaze with his. My stomach reeled when I thought about pretending to belong to Elijah. But, there it was. The only way out. The only way to get back to Luke and Mike.

"And what then? What if Eden won't leave? Do you plan to stay here and let him control you for the rest of your life because she won't go?"

Joseph's face fell at the prospect. "No. If she won't go with us, then I'll leave her here and get you home."

I picked up the papers and began reading over the details of my birth, my education, even my food preferences. The lies stretched on for pages, and I had to force myself to continue reading.

I prayed Joseph was telling the truth. If he wasn't . . . well, I had no problem leaving him behind.

TWENTY-ONE

The springs of the bed creaked loudly, probably the third time in the last few minutes Joseph had adjusted his position. I could practically feel his body tensing every time I turned a page. He was getting anxious, nervous about how long it was taking me to memorize my new life.

"Dee, it's been thirty minutes now. I know my father told you to memorize it, but as long as he knows you're trying, everything will be fine."

"I'm not taking any chances," I said, only half-believing myself. I needed to be as convincing as possible, and memorizing as much as I could would only make it easier.

I was approximately twenty pages deep into my made-up life when I stopped cold, the detailed timeline on the page startling me. "What is this?"

Joseph leaned over and gave the sheet a quick glance. "The history of Purity Springs."

"Not that," I said, brushing my hand over the two detailed paragraphs at the top of the page. "This."

I was staring at a timeline, a carefully maintained, handwritten timeline. Except this one didn't keep track of births or political events. This one cataloged every single illness ever to strike the US, right down to geographical location and death toll.

"Didn't you read the last two pages? The ones that explain why the original ten families of Purity Springs banded together in the first place?" Joseph asked.

"Ah ... no." I hadn't read the entire thing. I'd mostly looked for information on Rebekah and other key facts I'd have to know to pull this off. I didn't much care about the history of this insane town or the delusional reverend who'd founded it.

I circled back two pages and tried to read it again. It was worse than my AP History book. Not wanting to waste what little time I had left digesting this crap, I turned toward Joseph and said, "Give me the condensed version."

He took the papers from my hand and turned so that he was facing me. "Fine, but pay attention," he said, and I nodded. "August of 1854, Reverend Eli Smith Hawkins—"

"Relative of yours?" I asked, interrupting him.

"Yes, great-great-great-grandfather," he said, his hand waving in the air as he ticked off each generation. "He lived in the SoHo district of London. Broad Street to be exact. There was a cholera outbreak that summer, and he watched over one hundred and twenty of his neighbors die within three days. Like most kids back then, he grew up on the stories of the Black Death and smallpox, believed the outbreak was God's hand separating the evil from the good."

I chuckled at the "back then" comment. From where I was sitting, the people in this town were as ass-backward as their long-dead relatives. They still subscribed to all of that insane hand-of-evil crap.

Joseph leveled a glare at me, one that said *stop laughing and pay attention*. I did, and found myself running through my European history class in my head, trying to place the words "Black Death." I finally got it, and the haunting tune to "Ring Around the Rosie" invaded my brain as I recalled my limited knowledge of the plague.

"Eli did what most people had been told to do. He locked himself inside his home and kept the windows shut, refusing visitors. But when one of his wife's maids became violently ill, he decided to leave. He took twelve families from his congregation with him—only the strongest and healthiest, those who had shown no sign of illness—and came here."

"Fascinating," I said, rolling my eyes.

"They settled in New York City. Six months later, one entire family had been wiped out from yellow fever. Within a year, another one had been lost to scarlet fever. That's when Eli Hawkins moved the ten remaining families into the country, away from the sicknesses of the city and the evil surrounding his congregation."

Joseph flipped through the pages until he found the timeline I had questioned him about earlier. "Since then, the Hawkins family has kept track of each illness that has attacked the outside world. We viewed their downfall as proof that we are the chosen ones, the pure ones."

I scanned the timeline. Listed next to each disease was a date and the geographical location. Beside that was the death toll. *1918, Spanish flu, death toll: 500,000. 1952, polio, 57,628 cases reported.* I jumped several entries to the end. *2009, H1N1, death toll: 3,900.* From scarlet fever to chicken-pox to swine flu, they had every single disease cataloged. This was paranoia at its finest.

"What's this number mean?" I asked, pointing to the col-umn of zeroes that ran down the length of the page.

"That's the number of residents in Purity Springs who were infected by each particular illness."

"What!? You mean to tell me that not a single one of you has ever had the flu or strep throat, for God's sake?" It was ridiculous. There was no way this group of people, divine or not, had *never* been sick.

"No, we get sick. I mean, we've all gotten a fever or some-thing at some point in our lives, but we've all been spared from this," he said, tapping the paper.

"But I saw the graveyard. People *do* die here. Surely your father must acknowledge that?"

He nodded, a hint of frustration buried in his features. "He does, but most of them are old and ready to die anyway."

"You mother wasn't," I protested.

"No she wasn't," he said, a tinge of anger lacing his words. "And others have died young, but they're mostly women and children, followers of weak will."

People like me, I thought to myself. "And let me guess: your father uses this as proof to keep them all here, safe and free of the disease that lies beyond this town."

Joseph nodded. If I was reading him right, his look of confusion indicated that he didn't understand why I was having such a hard time swallowing any of this. I mean, why would I? The proof was right there in black and white. The pure had been spared while the weak of will perished.

"I had chickenpox when I was five," I said, pulling up the hem of my skirt to show my lone chickenpox scar on my left calf. "And I've had strep throat three times in the last five years. Does that make me impure enough to leave?"

Joseph smiled. It was sad and conciliatory, and I knew the answer before he spoke. "No. In his mind, that makes you stronger. It shows that you have the spirit and strength to survive. God spared your life when he could easily have taken it. My father won't see that as a curse. He'll see it as a blessing."

"Great," I said. "Lucky me."

TWENTY-TWO

I'd been alternating between disbelief and horror. Everyone here had been manipulated over time, their lives constructed by generations of lunatics.

And I was next in line to become one of them.

Joseph stood up and held out a hand for me to take. "You done reading?"

I could read these files all day and I still wouldn't be ready.

"Come on," he said, curling his fingers for me to take. "I promise that if you stick to the plan, it will all be fine."

Stacking the sheets together, I began mindlessly stuffing them back into the envelope. I'd been on overdrive since his father had left, racing frantically to come up with a better solution than the one I'd been handed. But nothing made any sense.

"I'm not stupid," Joseph said. "I know you think I'm

weird and nuts like my father, but I'm not. I'm also not the only one here who wants out."

I stopped wrestling with the papers and turned my attention to him. No, I didn't think he was stupid or even weird. I thought he was downright delusional. "You said yourself that everybody out there accepts what your father is preaching. Even if we can convince Elijah to let his guard down, there's no way these followers of his will simply let us walk out of here." I motioned toward the window. "You think they're just gonna let us take Eden and flip off everything your father stands for? Everything he's taught them to believe?"

Joseph sighed, the familiar look of exhaustion blanketing his features. "No. In fact, I'm sure my father will do everything in his power to make sure we stay."

"Exactly." My voice came out louder than I'd expected, not a hint of negotiation present in my tone. "I'm not stupid either, and I'm not naïve enough to think I can take him on alone."

"You're not alone." Joseph's expression was fierce, determined, but I didn't believe him for one second. I *was* alone. Without Luke and Mike to back me up, then I was completely, utterly alone.

"Even together, we can't win against him. This town follows his every command, practically worships him. Two against a town of one hundred forty-eight? Those odds suck," I said.

"Maybe, but it's not impossible. My Aunt Mary did it. My mother nearly made it. I did it myself, the day he killed her. We can do it too, Dee. We have to."

"In order for this to work, in order for use to even have a chance of getting Eden out of here, I need Luke and Mike."

"That's not—"

I flicked my hand in the air, stopping him. I didn't need to trust Joseph or memorize the contents of Elijah Hawkins's demented folder in order to survive. The only truth I'd come to realize during all this was that I needed Luke and his impulsive brother.

"I want them here. I don't believe you when you say they're safe. I want to see for myself." I paused briefly, then laid down an ultimatum of my own. "Besides, you said you were banking on them coming in here to get me out, right? I won't help you, Joseph, not unless you bring them here."

Joseph paced the edges of the room, his jaw set rigidly as he considered my demand. "They'll be in danger, you know. My father...he already knows about them. If he finds them, he'll kill them."

"He won't," I said, hoping I was right. "I won't let him."

The terror I'd been working so hard to reign in was back. I could see the main street through the window. The escape route we needed was so close, so damn close, but virtually impossible to reach.

Joseph stopped pacing and gave a quick nod. "Fine, but I can't go and get them. That would be way too obvious," he reasoned. "If I disappear again, my father will...well, let's say getting Eden out will be a non-issue."

"I'll go. You distract your father, and I'll go," I said.

"You're underestimating my father," Joseph said. "There's no way for you to slip out undetected."

My guess was he knew damn well I wouldn't come back for him. Any idiot would.

"So where does that leave us?" I asked, folding my arms across my chest. "I'm not helping you without Luke and Mike, and you're telling me that seeing them isn't gonna happen."

"I never said I wouldn't bring them here, only that neither you nor I are going to get them."

I was surprised I hadn't remembered it when I first woke up. The stalks swaying as we ran for the shack. The strange voices I heard when Luke tackled Joseph to the ground. And the pain exploding through my head. It wasn't Joseph who'd hit me. It was somebody else. "Oh my God. You weren't alone."

I remembered flashes of their two faces. They were both tall and skinny, not nearly as big as Luke or Joseph. But they'd managed to take me down and wrestle Mike and Luke back into that shed.

"Who are they?" I asked, fear overpowering my optimism. "Who were the other two kids with you?"

"Abram and James, and they want out as badly as me. Maybe more," he said. "Plus, they have someplace to go, someone waiting for them on the outside."

That statement brought my anger up short. Why would anybody with an alternative actually choose to stay here? "Then why are they still here?"

"They're my cousins. Three years younger than me. When the sirens went off and I didn't come back, they came looking for me. They didn't mean to hurt you, any of you.

But when they saw Luke on top of me, they thought…" Joseph trailed off.

His cousins had probably assumed Luke was going to kill Joseph, and they weren't exactly wrong.

"They want to come with me," Joseph continued. "They want to see their mother…my Aunt Mary."

"Why the hell didn't you tell me about them when you first woke up?" I was yelling now, angry and pissed that he'd kept this from me.

Joseph motioned for me to keep my voice down but I ignored him, not caring who heard me. We had four people outside these walls—four people who could help us—and yet he'd simply sat there, feeding me some stupid crap about playing along and trusting him.

"Go get them," I ordered. "Go tell them to let Luke and Mike go."

TWENTY-THREE

Alone all of three minutes, my heart was already hammering. Not from fear this time, but from anticipation. And hope. And excitement.

I'd purposefully avoided thinking about logistics. It was safer not to think about how two fourteen-year-old boys were going to sneak an understandably pissed-off Luke into my room. The mechanics of it all, the danger that seemed to follow our every move, were overwhelming.

The door opened, and I was across the room before I realized who it was. My entire world came crashing down when Joseph stepped in alone and softly closed the door behind him.

"Where are they?" I asked.

"James went to get them; he and Abram will bring them in through the back alleys."

"How long?" I glanced at the clock. It was nearly three already.

"Relax, Dee. It's going to take a bit of time. Too many people out and about. In a couple hours, the entire town will be in the chapel for evening prayer. That's the safest time to bring them in."

Evening prayer. And one messed-up meet-and-greet for me.

"But we're supposed to be *at* that service," I said, my voice rising with each passing breath. "That's why I'm dressed like this, so he can introduce me to his followers. It's the reason I had to memorize all that stuff and braid my hair and wash my makeup off and—"

Joseph cut me off with a hand to my shoulder. "I went to see my father before I came back. I told him you weren't feeling well and that even the simple task of braiding your hair seemed to take too much energy. I asked if we could delay your introduction till tomorrow, to give you time to rest."

"And he agreed?" I half expected Elijah to come barreling through the door, yank me to my feet, and demand that I perform.

"Not yet. He wants to see you for himself, so get in that bed and look sick."

I did as Joseph asked, going so far as to pull the elastic from my braid and yank a few strands free. Losing the clogs, I climbed under the quilt and bit down on my cheek until it bled. It worked. The taste of blood running down my throat made me nauseated. I considered scratching at my bandaged arms, hoping a bit of fresh blood might help make this whole lie believable. But I didn't get the chance. The soft knock on the door stopped me cold.

"Close your eyes," Joseph whispered as he dropped a wet cloth to my forehead. He looked tired and beaten-down himself, but I doubted that was an act.

Elijah slid into the room, the mattress shifting as Joseph relinquished his place on the bed to his father. "Rebekah," Elijah whispered, his hand trailing to my hair. "Joseph tells me that you aren't feeling well."

I turned my head toward Elijah's voice and opened my eyes, fluttering them twice for effect. I had a lot of practice playing sick, although it usually preceded a chemistry test I hadn't studied for or a detention I didn't want to sit through.

"I have brought you something I think will help you see more clearly," Elijah said.

He pulled a ribbon-tied box from his coat pocket and placed it on the nightstand next to my bed. Judging from the size and shape, I gathered it was a wedding band, which meant I wasn't planning on opening it. Ever.

He caught me watching it and deliberately pushed it aside. "I was hoping to introduce you to my following tonight. The sooner we start our new life together, the easier this will be."

I moaned rather than answered. Probably safer, given that the only words I could possibly string together were violent curses.

"Father," Joseph said, "she truly isn't well."

"Rebekah?" Elijah soothed. The door to my room clicked

again, and I wondered who else he'd summoned to help him break me down. "Rebekah, dear, can you look at me?"

I opened my eyes wider, my mind racing to figure out what was up with the sudden affection. I quickly remembered it had nothing to do with me, that he was the same maniacal man I'd met earlier. This was nothing more than a cover for the benefit of the young girl who'd slipped into the room and was standing next to him.

She tipped her head slightly as she stared down at me, a mixture of confusion and curiosity sparkling in her eyes. They were brown like her brother's, and huge, but they lacked the hopelessness I'd come to associate with Joseph's gaze. Her body was willowy, her hair neatly braided, and she kept sending hesitant glances back toward Elijah, smiling when she finally got his attention.

I didn't need a formal introduction. I'd have known this girl anywhere. Eden.

Joseph instinctually slid his body in front of hers, a protective gesture he'd probably done a thousand times before. I liked it. It reminded me a little of Luke.

"You understand why it is important for Joseph to go to evening services with me tonight?" Elijah asked as he took the damp cloth from my forehead and dropped it into the basin. He wrung it out and checked its temperature against his own wrist before smoothing it back over my forehead. "I hate to leave you alone, but it is crucial that Joseph show his support for me and the gift I've been blessed with."

My eyes moved to Joseph. He nodded, confirming my thoughts. I was the gift.

"But I don't think it's wise to leave you alone," Elijah continued as he placed a gentle hand under my chin and guided my eyes to his. "Being that you are so weak, I have asked my daughter, Eden, to sit with you."

Eden's eyes barely made contact with mine before skirting back to the floor, her voice a whisper as she said, "Hello."

Unlike the bland garments I'd been forced to wear, Eden's clothes consisted of a knee-length beige skirt and a rather bright blue shirt. I wouldn't say she was fashionable or even looked good; rather, she was more like the awkward, smart girl who sat at the back of class. We had one. Every school had one. Her name was Kerry, or Kaylan, or Kaitlin or something. I'd never paid her much attention; now I'd give anything for the chance to ask her what her name was.

I went to sit up, then remembered I was playing sick. Groaning, I slumped back down. In an effort to help me, Elijah slid one arm around my back and the other under my knees. He lifted me up, repositioning me so I had a better view of the room. Of Eden. Of him.

"Are you sick?" she asked me.

Yes," I said, following her eyes to the floor. I caught the movement of her hand against the pocket of her skirt. It was trimmed with satin, the small patch she was working between her fingers nearly gone.

Twelve. Joseph said she was twelve, but sitting here, watching Eden twist her hands in her skirt, she looked more like seven. And if that was the case, if she was as sheltered and naïve as Joseph had said, then she was screwed.

"I'll be okay," I said and held out my hand. "It's nice to finally meet you."

Eden waved shyly, every last bit of her innocence shining through in that gesture. I was way younger than her when I'd realized the world essentially sucked. But then again, I had other kids to compare myself to. All Eden had was a town full of blind followers.

"Joseph is worried about you," she said, reaching out for her brother. Joseph took her hand and squeezed gently. Eden turned her attention to her father and gave him the same adoring gaze. "I can sit with her if you want. That way she won't be alone during evening services."

This was perfect. Joseph and I couldn't have planned this better if we'd tried. No need to pretend to submit to Elijah's divine authority. With only Eden in the room and Elijah tied up preaching that "wrath of God" crap to his followers, Eden and I could be out of this place in no time. No one to stop us. No one to even see us escape. I sent a quick look Joseph's way, and he jerked his head in agreement.

"I'd like that," I said. Soon, Luke, Mike, and I would have Eden miles from here. Joseph would just have to catch up with us later.

"Eden knows to come and find me should you become physically ill," Elijah said. "I have explained to her that you are a bit confused and weak. She is also aware that you have been isolated since your birth, and that the idea of being introduced to the community is a bit overwhelming for you. She will come and get me if you become overly agitated or start speaking nonsense."

His words required nothing more than a nod of understanding, but I wouldn't give him that. I knew full well that his phony kindness was nothing more than a warning in disguise. Eden wasn't to be my caretaker; she was to be my guard, and one false move on my part would send her running straight to him.

Elijah took my silence for agreement and leaned in to place a kiss on my cheek. "Good girl."

He was in the midst of motioning Joseph toward the door when someone knocked. The knob spun to the right, then stopped, as if whoever was out there was waiting for permission to enter.

"Expecting someone?" Elijah asked.

The color drained from my cheeks as I searched my mind for something to do ... something to say to prevent the inevitable. Joseph had that same look of terror on his face, was grasping at the same dead air as me.

"Answer it," Elijah said as he took a seat on the bed. He stretched his legs out casually and grinned. "We've got plenty of time before I'm expected at the altar, and I would love to speak with your guests."

Out of options, Joseph went to the door, his hand tensing on the knob as he twisted it. My eyes glanced over the two boys who came in. Twins. Identical, down to the small mole to the right of their mouths and the tinge of red in their hair. I had hazy memories of them from the morning—their hands, the rough feel of their shirts, and the log to the back of my head.

I shrugged off those thoughts, too busy searching the

space behind them for Luke and Mike. Holding my breath, I waited for them to walk through the door, wanting nothing more than to see them, yet hoping they weren't there. I prayed they'd somehow escaped and were already heading home for help.

"They're not—"

It was the sound of the unfamiliar voice that forced me to start breathing again. "No," I shouted, cutting them off.

They both swung their heads in my direction, following my eyes to Elijah.

"Abram. James," Elijah said and stood up. They bowed their heads and locked their hands together at their backs. "Your father is waiting for you in the chapel. I haven't told him about your plans or your involvement with all of this, only that I think you need to spend some time, as a family, reflecting on your mother's sins. I hate to think what he'd do if he knew."

A shiver worked its way through each of them, the same fear settling into me. I went to say something, to covertly ask them where Luke and Mike were, but Elijah saw my open mouth and cut me off.

"Eden, darling, please go along with Abram and James to the chapel. I will be along shortly—I wish to speak to your brother and Rebekah alone."

Eden didn't argue; she simply got up and followed Abram and James to the door. I caught the quick glance they sent Joseph's way.

"Go," Joseph said, trying to reassure his cousins. "We'll be there soon."

The sound of the knob catching brought with it a terrifying knowledge. My plan—finding Luke and Mike and dragging Eden out of here while Elijah was tied up at the evening service—had unraveled before it even had a chance to start.

"I have changed my mind," Elijah said. He may have been looking at Joseph, but his words were directed squarely at me. "I think it's best if Rebekah meets our family sooner rather than later. There's no point in waiting. No reason to put off the inevitable."

That truth had me shaking, inching myself farther away from Elijah as I tried to meld myself with the wall.

"I'll expect the two of you to join me promptly at five," Elijah continued as he made his way to the door. "And don't forget your gift. I took special care picking out the right one for you. I had ten to choose from, but this one spoke to me."

I stared at the box, all pure and white with the thin blue ribbon tied around it. "Go ahead," Elijah prompted. "Open it up. I want to see your joy when you understand how deeply my commitment to you runs."

Hesitantly, I picked up the box. It felt uncomfortable in my fingers, bomb-like as I turned it over and inspected the ribbon. I lifted my gaze to Elijah. He had a look of sheer pleasure on his face.

"What's inside?" I asked.

"A small token to guide your future actions," he replied. "Now open it."

I held the box out for Elijah to take back and said, "No thank you."

Elijah shook his head slowly, refusing to take it.

"Father," Joseph started to say, but a caustic glare from Elijah quickly shut him up.

Joseph moved, then, firmly planting himself between his father and me. I should've felt safer with him blocking Elijah's moves, but I didn't. I'd seen Joseph's scars, knew damn well that Elijah would go through Joseph to get to me if that's what it took.

The air between us grew suffocating, and I willed myself to stay calm as I dropped the box to the floor. "I don't want it."

The kindness slid from Elijah's face, leaving behind a mask of cold, hard features. In one swift movement, he picked the box up and crushed it into my palm. The edges were sharp, and I bit my tongue rather than cry out as he twisted it into my hand. The corner dug into my palm, piercing the skin. A tiny drop of blood marred the white cardboard. Elijah grinned, pressing down harder until I cried out and tried to jerk my hand away.

Elijah was quick, quicker than Joseph. By the time Joseph realized what his father was doing, Elijah was already on top of me, digging his fingers into my upper arm in an attempt to hold me still.

Joseph put a hand on his father's shoulder. His fingers flexed and the tendons in his arm tightened in preparation. "Let her go," he demanded, and Elijah slowly pulled back.

"I wouldn't do that, boy. My tolerance for your disobedience is wearing thin, and I'd hate to have to make a permanent change to your position within our family," Elijah threatened.

"I won't let you hurt her," Joseph replied, his voice oddly calm given who he was challenging.

"I promise you, Joseph, she is not the one who will suffer. Now take your hands off me."

Joseph stood strong, with no hint of giving in to his father's command. In fact, he widened his stance and clenched his free hand into a fist.

"Please, don't," I said, begging Joseph to let it go. I'd open the box and put on whatever piece of jewelry Elijah wanted me to if it meant keeping the peace. I just needed Joseph to back down before everything blew up in my face.

Reluctantly, Joseph let go and Elijah reminded me of his original demand: "I told you to open it. *Now.*"

Elijah's voice was nothing more than a growl as he wrapped his own fingers around mine and squeezed until I thought they would break. My index finger was bent sideways around the box, the angle so unnatural that a sharp pain shot up my wrist, forcing a gasp from my lips. It was only then, when Elijah had vocal confirmation of my pain, that he eased up and stepped back.

I fumbled with the wrapping paper, my eyes closing briefly as I braced myself for the first sparkle of the ring he was undoubtedly going to make me wear. The ring that would further mark me as his and a possession of this crazy town filled with equally crazy people. I carefully peeled back the tissue paper and stared down at what looked like skin.

TWENTY-FOUR

My eyes faded in and out of focus as the finger took shape. A bloody, human finger. The stump was ragged, the tiniest bit of white bone showing through the mangled flesh. Fresh blood coated the satin bottom of the jewelry box, seeping into the white tissue paper it was cradled in, dying it red.

I gasped and dropped the box. The finger rolled out, sliding across the floor, leaving a thin trail of blood behind. I pulled a hand to my mouth in an attempt to keep the contents of my stomach from spewing out.

"Whose finger is that?" I choked out.

Elijah chuckled. "You don't honestly need me to answer that, do you?" His tone was so even, so balanced, that he sounded more like the manager of a Taco Bell than the psychopath I knew he was. "You're obviously a smart girl.

You've managed to convince my son to do your bidding and allowed him to take a beating that was rightfully yours."

"She didn't do anything," Joseph interrupted. He wedged his body between me and his father. There was barely an inch of space between us, but Joseph took up every bit of it, pressing me into his back, protecting me. "She has nothing to do with me leaving. Nothing to do with me or Mom or Aunt Mary. You leave her out of this."

"Don't patronize me, Joseph. I know exactly what you've been doing, both of you."

I peered around Joseph's shoulder, forcing myself to look down at the finger. What had he meant by "you don't need me to answer that"? I squinted, suddenly realizing there was a mark on the finger I hadn't seen when it was in the box. A tiny black mark. A tattoo.

I inhaled sharply, staring at it. The barest hint of ink took shape, the black marks stroking downward three times. I inched closer, tears streaming down my face as the tiny Roman numeral three came into view.

"Oh my God. Oh my God!" I shrieked.

I wracked my brain, tried frantically to remember if the ink on Luke's tattoo was that dark, if the lines were that narrow. I could see his hands clear as day—the calloused palms and the cracked knuckles from playing ball in the cold. I could trace every seam of his fingers and knew that the pinky on his left hand was bent at the tip, broken courtesy of an offensive guard two seasons ago. And the middle finger on his left hand ... that one was inked with a tattoo.

"This is…this is Luke's?" I was barely able to get the words out. Spots flashed before my eyes as I fought to breathe.

A twisted smirk spread across Elijah's face. He was happy, enjoying every second of my agony. All this time I'd thought Luke and Mike were tucked safely away in that shack, and now I knew the truth. He'd found them, tortured them, and that knowledge was splintering me into a thousand different pieces all at once.

"What did you do?" I scrambled out from behind Joseph and hurled myself at Elijah, tearing into him like I was possessed.

Elijah stumbled backward, stunned, and I lunged at him again, intent on getting my nails into the soft spot on his neck, into his jugular. I was going to kill him. Screw saving Eden. I was going to kill Elijah Hawkins here and now, and then I was going to walk out of here.

"I warned you!" Elijah yelled as he grabbed a fistful of my hair and pulled me off him. He yanked my head back so that I was looking at him. His breath was hot as he pressed his face next to mine, his mouth touching my ear. "I told you to do *exactly* as I said. When you disobey me, there are consequences."

His voice lowered as his disgusting, sour breath poured out over me. He kicked Luke's finger closer to me, forcing me to look at it. "We don't desecrate our bodies here. They are our temples, and this mark, this *disfigurement*, was a sin. It had to be removed or he had no chance of salvation. Trust me, he will thank me for this one day. Both of you will."

My mind flashed frantically to Luke's initials inked on my

tailbone. I'd gotten that tattoo four months ago when we were drunk and feeling invincible. We'd driven two hours to Canada and ended up in some sketchy tattoo parlor that didn't think twice about verifying our fake IDs. Luke held my hand as the needle dug into my skin again and again, branding us as belonging to each other. Exactly how did Elijah plan on getting rid of that?

I clawed at Elijah with both hands, tried to fend him off despite his hand fisted in my hair. In one swift motion, he released his hold on me and gave me a hard shove. I landed on the floor, my elbow breaking my fall.

Joseph ran for me, my name—my real name—tumbling from his lips. Elijah hauled off and slapped him, sending Joseph stumbling backward, away from me.

"Stay out of this, Joseph," he ordered, then crouched down next to me, his lips inches from mine as he jerked my chin up, forcing me to hear, to digest, each word he said. "You listen carefully, because I will not remind you again. You will not cross me. You will not disobey me, and you will not refuse me. If you do, I promise someone you love will suffer. At the end of the day, you will be safe and warm in my care. You will be guided by me. Your salvation will come through me. It is that boy who will pay. Have I made myself clear?"

When I didn't answer, he shook me hard. "I asked you a question, Rebekah. I expect an answer."

Joseph crawled up next to me, his hand cradling the side of his face. "Stop it!"

"Or what, Joseph?" The veins in Elijah's forehead pulsed as he dared his son to do anything but back down. "You want to try something? Go ahead. Do it. But rest assured, I know all your weaknesses. I know exactly how to get you to do what I want."

I'd been here less than a day, and even I could read between Elijah's twisted lines. He'd figured out why Joseph had come back, why he'd brought me back. Eden.

"Perhaps a little persuasion is needed where you are concerned as well," Elijah said as he stood up. "You're sister is young, Joseph. She has so much life ahead of her, a life that could be perfectly comfortable here. But that's up to you."

"Don't you touch her," Joseph growled, the panic he'd kept so well hidden flaming in his eyes. He looked helpless, and I found myself wondering how many beatings he'd taken for Eden, how many times he'd bared his own flesh to spare hers.

"Your aunt, your mother, even this girl here has paid the price for your indiscretions. Shall we make Eden pay as well? Because it will be your hands that bear her blood and your soul that is condemned, not mine. I don't kill my followers. They choose their own fate, and in turn, their own punishment."

I wanted nothing more than for Joseph to hit Elijah, to knock him on the ground and pummel him. But I knew he wouldn't. He had at least fifty pounds on his father and was a good three inches taller, not to mention younger and stronger. There was nothing stopping him from knocking Elijah out right now, except for the threat to Eden.

Elijah smoothed out the wrinkles on the front of his shirt and shot a look of disgust in Joseph's direction. "You're lucky, son. This town has been run by our family for generations, and if you weren't next in line to take over..."

He paused and looked at me, his eyes carrying a promise that made my skin crawl. "Tread lightly, Joseph, because once this girl here gives me another son to fashion in my own likeness, I will have no need for you." A smug smile crept across his face. "No wonder your boyfriend is so worried about you. You're a very stupid girl."

I swiped at the tears slipping down my cheeks, horrible images flickering in my mind. Luke tied up. Luke without a finger. Luke bleeding and worrying about me. Mike screaming for help. Joseph struggling to stand up straight as his father took a belt to his back. And me stuck here forever.

"Shut up!" I yelled.

Elijah chuckled once more as reached for the doorknob "This time I took one marred finger. Next time I'll take his hand. Keep disobeying me, *Rebekah*, and soon I'll have his life."

TWENTY-FIVE

I stood there staring up at the golden cross glinting in the fading daylight. It flashed like a beacon against the dusk. I rubbed my upper arms briskly, hoping to ward off the chill that was quickly making its way through my thin cotton shirt. No use; the bitter cold had settled into my bones the second I saw Luke's finger.

My head was throbbing and my mind was one steady stream of incoherent thoughts. Truth was, I couldn't remember a damn thing about the past few hours. I remembered the jewelry box, Elijah laughing, and Luke's finger, but nothing else. I'd gone numb, placed one foot in front of the other, and walked toward the front door of the chapel, staring into a future that looked bleaker by the moment.

I gripped the railing by the outside steps, its frigid metal bringing me back to the present. Elijah was standing at the top of the steps, smiling and clapping an older man on the back. I couldn't hear what they were saying, but they looked at ease with each other, grinning as they spoke.

"It's going to be okay, Dee," Joseph whispered.

His hand brushed against mine, and I pulled away. "Leave me alone."

I blamed Joseph for this. If he hadn't run off. If he hadn't set off the alarms. If he hadn't approached us that morning. If he hadn't been so intent on saving his sister. All these *what ifs* leading me back to where I was...stuck. "This is your fault, you know. Your stupid, idiotic, selfish plan has ruined all our lives."

A car pulled alongside the chapel, and Joseph tensed beside me. I ignored the man exiting the driver's side and followed Joseph's gaze to the passenger side, my eyes trailing from the man's polished boots to his crisp pants to the gun holstered at his side. I kept going, my heart catching in my throat when I saw his shiny silver badge.

A tiny bit of hope surfaced as I took in his brown uniform. The Hoopers must have sensed something was wrong when I didn't call last night and notified the police. Or maybe somebody passing by heard the sirens or saw our mangled car and called it in. Perhaps Mike had gotten away. Propelled by my own stupid optimism, I lunged forward. If I could only get his attention.

Joseph gripped my forearm, hard. I was about to shake him off when the look on his face stopped me cold.

"What?" I asked.

A tight nod of his head told me I wasn't seeing what I thought I was. "My uncles," he said.

"Jared. Jacob. So good of you to come," Elijah called out, his voice loud and startling as if he intended it to carry my way. "As you know, this is a very important day for both me and our family."

Joseph released my arm and moved so I'd have a clear view of his uncles. "They're not here to help you, Dee. They're not here to help any of us."

Both men bowed their heads. "We wouldn't miss it for the world, Elijah," the officer said as he pulled a large envelope from the inside of his jacket. The second man followed suit, producing a smaller one from his briefcase. He was dressed impeccably, in a suit and a pale blue shirt. He looked more like a banker than a small-town councilman.

"Never late with your share, are you, brothers?"

Elijah hugged them both and motioned to two women and half a dozen kids standing on the chapel's front lawn. The kids came rushing forward, chanting the word "Daddy" as they each found some part of the men to cling to. Their wives followed behind quietly. I watched as each man carefully extricated a hand and held it out to his wife. The look of complete adoration and utter happiness on the women's faces made me sick.

"*Brothers*," I groaned. They weren't my hope. They were another dead end.

Elijah turned back to face us, and the sheriff's eyes traveled past him and landed on me. Every muscle in my body tensed as the man's smile widened. Apparently, he approved of Elijah's choice of brides. Well, screw him.

"Rebekah, it's time," Elijah said, beckoning me forward.

I swallowed hard rather than say something that would get Luke hurt even more.

Elijah opened the doors wide and the entire congregation turned to see me. I quickly ran through the math in my head as I walked down the center aisle, impressed that I still had the presence of mind to do simple calculations. There were twenty pews, ten on each side. I counted the heads of the people in the row to my left. Eight—nine if you counted the infant bundled into his mother's arms.

My mind quickly flashed back to the signs in the maintenance shed. One fifty? No, one forty-nine. Minus Joseph's mom made it one-forty eight. Elijah could fit the whole damn town in this chapel, and judging from the cramped space, he'd done just that.

"Your seat, my dear," Elijah said as he guided me down into the hard wooden pew. "I'll be introducing you shortly, so keep in mind everything we discussed. This would be a very bad time for you to become defiant. Bad for you; worse for your friends. Understood?"

I nodded mechanically as he walked away, then looked up and down both sides of the room for an exit. Other than the door we'd come through, I found nothing. Not that I'd have a prayer of getting out of here anyway. Not with a hundred and forty-eight eerily faithful servants blocking my way.

The front of the sanctuary held a long table. Scattered across it were a few leather-bound books, three pillar candles, and a book of matches. Off to the side was a podium with a plaque bolted to its front. I had to squint to make out the words *past*, *present*, and *future*.

I watched as Elijah's brother, the councilman, walked up and began lighting the candles one at a time. He'd changed his clothes. Gone was the fancy suit and tie; in its place were the same plain black pants and white shirt everybody else was wearing. I swiveled around and searched the congregation for the sheriff. He was heading down the center aisle. No gun, no uniform, just the same ugly, Purity Springs-issued prison suit.

Joseph slipped into the row across the aisle, looking past me to wink at his sister. His face was tense, his eyes dark as he mouthed the words "I'm sorry" to me. I looked away. He wasn't sorry. He was guilty, and I wasn't about to help ease his conscience.

Elijah tapped on the altar. That tiny noise sent the room into complete silence, and he dropped his head in prayer. I watched as everybody followed suit, their heads dipping down and their lips whispering in unison. Chills raced up my arms as the hushed voices closed in around me. I kept my eyes on Eden, frantically trying to figure out what she was chanting.

Joseph coughed, and I looked up to see Elijah staring down at me. I smiled, playing along, and he returned his attention back to his congregation.

"You look afraid. Are you?"

I turned toward Eden's whispered words. Her huge eyes looked worried, her fingers rubbing the same satin-lined pocket as before.

I looked up to make sure Elijah was fully immersed in

his prophesying duties before I whispered back, "A little. Are you?"

Sitting there, watching her rub that small spot of fabric like a child, I began to understand why Joseph was willing to risk his life for her. Eden didn't stand a chance, and with their mother gone, Joseph was her only hope.

Eden kept her eyes focused forward as she quickly shook her head. "No, I'm not scared. Most of the time I'm just lonely." Her fingers disappeared into the pocket of her skirt and she pulled out what looked like a piece of dried corn husk.

"Whatcha got there?" I whispered.

"Joseph made it for me," Eden said shyly. Her eyes lit up. It was the tiniest flicker of adoration, and it only lasted a second, but it was enough for me to know she worshipped her brother. "We're not supposed to have toys, but Joseph said every little girl needs a doll."

She inched the small figure closer to me, holding it out as if giving me permission to inspect it. I turned my head slightly and caught a glimpse of Joseph. He bowed his head, motioning for me to do the same. He had no idea what his sister and I were talking about, and that made his gentle nod in our direction that much sweeter.

"Can I see it?" I asked.

Eden laid the doll down on the pew between us, rearranging her skirt to keep it hidden. I ran my fingers across the ball at the top. It was dry, the husks aging and beginning to peel away. Joseph had used ink to fashion eyes. There was a mouth, too, but it was nearly gone, faded from use. Around the doll was a scrap of white fabric. It was nothing more than a rectangle with a notch cut out for the head and a piece of twine cinched around what was supposed to be a waist, but it served its purpose.

"I have more," she said as she pulled out two more pieces of fabric—light blue and black. I couldn't help but smile. Joseph had made her a doll, complete with an interchangeable wardrobe.

Eden caught my expression and nudged the doll in my direction. "She makes you happy."

It wasn't the doll so much as it was Joseph. Despite who his father was and all he'd been forced to endure, he could still be kind and gentle when it came to his sister. "Yes. She's very pretty."

"Then you keep her," Eden said.

"I couldn't," I responded, thinking I would rather die than take this girl's only toy. "Joseph made her for you. She belongs with you."

"He can make me another." Eden picked the doll up and felt around my skirt until she found the pocket. Her fingers worked quickly, and before I could argue, she had the doll safely tucked inside.

I didn't know what to say. *Thank you* didn't seem to be enough. She was a little girl with no mother and a head-case for a father; the only good thing in her life was Joseph, and he was forced to risk his own safety to make her a doll. I never imagined I'd think it, but even my past paled in comparison to this.

I clenched my eyes shut, my resolve wavering. I hadn't

expected this, hadn't planned on saving anybody but myself and Luke and Mike. But I knew I wouldn't leave her behind now. I couldn't.

TWENTY-SIX

"Rebekah."

The name floated through the air, but I didn't register it as my own. Joseph stood up and backed out of his own pew before motioning for me to get up.

"Dee, go," he whispered.

Elijah's hand was outstretched in an act of kindness, but his eyes promised retribution should I do anything to step out of my role. My feet felt like lead as I climbed the steps, my eyes never meeting his. He grasped my shoulders as I reached him and turned me around to face the congregation.

I looked to the back of the room, where three large woo-den crosses hung above the entrance. A trio of silver bowls—not unlike the one I'd seen overflowing with my own blood—sat atop a table near the door.

My eyes flicked to the words inscribed on Elijah's podium.

Past, present, and *future.* I wasn't a particularly religious person. The way I saw it, God had given up on me the day I was born. But after suffering through a few masses with the Hoopers, even I knew that those words referred to more than verb tense. They referred to the three divisions of time, and sometimes to prophecies.

Prophecies.

I closed my eyes and reopened them, hoping that things would look different, that I wouldn't be staring at an entire room filled with the number three.

I swiveled around to face the candles flickering behind me. Three separate and distinct flames danced in and out of each other's paths. I stiffened as the final realization slammed into me. There were three of us stuck here. Three of us who were supposed to be on a three-day trip.

And tomorrow... tomorrow would be day three.

I was going crazy. I had to be, because the thoughts racing through my mind were completely illogical. Impossible. Luke's obsession with the number three had nothing to do with what was happening. *Nothing.*

Elijah was still talking, his not-so-gentle squeeze of my hand reminding me to stay in the game.

Most of the congregation was on their feet, clapping. I hadn't heard Elijah's introduction, but judging from his followers' reactions, they obviously approved of me. Of course they would. He could tell them all to drink battery acid and they would blindly oblige.

The applause died out and Joseph sat back down, mouthing the words "It's all right" to me as he tried for a reassuring look. I didn't need reassurance, but the fact that *he* thought I did had me taking a second look at Elijah.

Elijah's brother—the sheriff this time—stood up and made his way to the back of the church. He collected three silver bowls and a long white scarf before making his way back toward me.

Everything seemed to be happening in slow motion, each movement around me deliberate and methodical. The three empty bowls were placed on the altar, and then Elijah carefully undid the button on the cuff of his shirt, his eyes never leaving mine as he rolled up his right sleeve.

"Smile, my love. This is the most important day of your life," Elijah said as he grabbed my arm and pushed the sleeve of my shirt to my elbow.

The most important day of my life? I surveyed the faces staring at me. They all looked expectant, full of joy and promise. "I don't understand," I murmured.

Elijah's hand lingered in the crook of my arm, his fingers tracing the veins leading to by wrist. With a nod to his brother, he grabbed onto my hand and turned it so my palm lay face up inside his. "Jared, would you please?"

His brother placed the white scarf over my forearm and wrapped it around twice, attaching the other end to Elijah the same way.

Elijah took one large step back toward the altar, our bound wrists forcing me to move with him. Then he leaned in, his free hand cupping the side of my cheek. "Today I will tie you to me in every way possible."

I shook my head, the horror of what he was saying

settling in. "You said this was about me meeting your family, about introducing me to your followers," I choked out.

"I *am* introducing you … as my wife."

I went to yank my hand free. "Don't," Elijah said. "Remember, it won't be you who suffers, but your friends."

He side-stepped me over to where his other brother was shifting the bowls, aligning them perfectly beneath our bound wrists. It wasn't until I saw the knife that everything finally clicked into place.

There weren't going to be any traditional wedding vows. That would be too easy. Too normal. No, Elijah was going to blood-oath us; slit both our palms and mingle our blood so that our spirits, our essences, combined.

Terror took over as I fought back the urge to scream. Elijah placed a hand on my shoulder, gently stroking it like I was a skittish animal. He was fully enthroned in his role now—the charming, kind, strong-hearted leader of this great community.

"Easy, Rebekah," he soothed.

The gentle tone of his voice had me shaking in fear, and I lost it. I jerked my wrist so hard that the fabric tore in two, the sheer force sending me stumbling backward. One of his brothers caught me and eased me upright, then gently nudged me in Elijah's direction.

Elijah's eyes were a shade of deadly I'd never seen before. His face was contorted, twisted and torn between anger and staying in character. It took him a second to regain his composure, but he finally did, the charming façade sliding back into place.

"I know you are frightened," he said loudly enough for his followers to hear. "But you are amongst family now. There is nothing to fear."

He circled his hand around the back of my neck and leaned in, his hushed words whispering across my ear. "Shall we try this again without the theatrics, Rebekah?"

I felt his thumb gently caress the side of my neck. It was a suggestive gesture, one Luke had done to me a thousand times. One that always ended in the same way—me on my back with Luke smiling down from above.

I smiled, and then knew in that instant that Elijah thought he'd won. His bad. "I'd rather lie with the devil than ever, *ever*, let you touch me."

Elijah chuckled and dug his fingers into the back of my neck, dragging me closer until my lips met his. "Keep it up, little girl, and that's exactly who you will be sleeping with."

TWENTY-SEVEN

Some things you don't need to see to believe because deep down, in the very core of your being, you know they're true. And I knew, without a shadow of a doubt, that Elijah wasn't simply capable of sending me to the devil ... he was the devil.

His grip on my neck loosened, and his hand moved to my waist. Pinpricks of sweat beaded up on his forehead, a sign that, if nothing else, I was at least making things difficult for him. Good. It wasn't much, but it was something.

"Again," Elijah said to his brother as he refastened the scarf to my wrist. It was shorter now, nearly half the length, so the binding was tighter.

"Hold still," he said.

The velvet nature of his voice was gone, his words curt and full of warning. The sharp glint of the blade sent ripples of fear through me, and I searched the crowd for Joseph. I may have blamed him for everything that had happened...was still happening. But in the end, he was the closest thing I had to an ally in here, and I needed him.

"Rebekah?" Elijah's gaze swept between Joseph and me. He'd seen my silent plea for help. "You can't be that naïve. You think I don't see the way you look at him? The way he looks at you? I know why he left that day. Know exactly why he dragged you back here with him. He can't save you *or* Eden. He doesn't have that kind of power. Only I do."

Turning toward his followers, Elijah cleared his throat and announced, "The rite to perform the marriage ceremony is reserved for those of the highest realm—myself and my brothers. This ritual has ensured the purity of our bloodline, not only by binding wife to husband, but also by binding the couple to this community."

Hell no, I thought to myself. Elijah wasn't interested in binding husband to wife. The only thing he was interested in was binding everybody in this town to him.

"Today we break from that tradition," he continued, and I shifted my weight, wondering what he had in store for me now. "Today my son, Joseph, the future of our prophecy, of Purity Springs, will have the honor of performing this most sacred of our rituals.

The color drained from Joseph's face as he rose slowly from his pew and walked toward us.

"Please," I choked out. "Let one of your brothers do it."

Elijah placed a finger to my lips, silencing me. "You think he won't hurt you, that it is *you* who controls *him*?" he asked. "Joseph is my son. *My son.* He may have flashes of his mother's weak will, but he was raised by me. Molded by me. You'd be wise to remember that."

My heart stopped as I processed his words. If I couldn't trust Joseph, then I was screwed. Literally screwed.

"On the other hand," Elijah continued, his hand brushing away the tears streaming down my face, "I'm not the monster you're making me out to be. Should you cooperate, I'll give you an hour with your friend. An hour to say goodbye to the boy who drove in here with you. Perhaps such a kindness on my part will enable you to put your past behind you for good."

Hope surged through me. I didn't care that Elijah only offered because he needed me to cooperate or because his precious followers believed I was the eager virgin-bride he'd made me out to be. All that mattered was that I was going to get to see Luke.

"Do you understand what I am proposing, Rebekah?" he asked.

I swallowed down a strangled sob and nodded. It took all of two seconds for me to extend my arm and accept his hideous offer. An ounce of my blood for an hour with Luke, for the possibility of escaping... yeah, I'd do that.

Elijah grasped my hand and pressed our forearms together. "Are we ready?

"I'm ready," I said, and the congregation rose to their feet, all eyes watching him. Watching me.

"Do not be afraid, Rebekah. With the Lord's help, my

strong and capable hands will guide us both through this union."

A confident smirk played across Elijah's lips as he took the knife from his brother's hand and held it out for Joseph to take. Joseph hesitated, his hands trembling as he reached for the blade.

"Shallow, Joseph," Elijah said. "We are not trying to cleanse, merely bind."

Joseph laid the blade across his father's palm and I willed him to slice deep, to spill every last drop of Elijah's disgusting blood. He carefully drew the blade back, a thin trail of red welling up against his father's skin.

Elijah smiled in approval and fisted his hand, the motion producing a small stream of blood that trickled down his hand to where our wrists were bound together. The blood was so dark it looked like ink, like the purplish black of the night sky before a storm. I fixed my eyes on it as it flowed, the warmth of it horrifying and nauseating.

I held back a whimper as the blade touched my skin. I could see Elijah's blood tainting the metal, warm and wet against the palm of my hand.

"I'm sorry," Joseph whispered, but I didn't respond. *Sorry* wasn't going to do either of us any good now.

Blinking back tears, I looked at Joseph and silently gave him my permission. He needed to do this. For Luke. For Mike. For Eden, he needed to do this.

TWENTY-EIGHT

I forced myself to stay silent and remain expressionless as Joseph drew the knife across from my skin. I could feel him watching me, his desperation building as he tried to make eye contact, but I kept my eyes on the floor, not capable of handling his guilt.

Crimson rose to the surface and began spilling out, mingling with Elijah's blood before dripping down onto the ground. The cut Joseph made was small, only about an inch in length, but it hurt like hell.

"Can you feel that, Rebekah? It's the union. The union of our blood and our spirits becoming one."

Elijah flexed his hand one last time, sending another trickle of blood running down my wrist.

"The bowl, please," Elijah said as he lifted his arm. The motion dragged mine upward with his. Joseph moved instantly, grabbing the largest bowl and placing it beneath our joined wrists. Drops of blood collected in its shiny metal bottom, the barely audible sound exploding through my ears.

Elijah began slowly unwrapping our arms. He laid the red-stained scarf in a second, more ornate bowl, and a fleeting thought crossed my mind. Would he keep this little memento of our marriage? Was his plan to bring it out on our first anniversary, like most people did with the top of their wedding cake?

"Holy water," Elijah said.

Joseph handed him the crystal bottle, and Elijah poured it into the last of the silver bowls. He took a clean towel from Jared and soaked it through before pressing it to my arm. I winced at the pain and he gentled his movements, a tiny smile parting his lips.

"You have done well," he soothed, applying pressure to my bleeding hand. He turned to Joseph, and for a split second I swore I saw pride in Elijah's eyes. "Excellent job, my son. If you'd like to make the announcement, we'll adjourn. It's time for Rebekah to meet my following."

"What?" I asked, anger flaming into my cheeks. "But you promised me that right after—"

"I'm a man of my word, Rebekah. I said I'd let you see your friend, and I will, but your new family comes first."

I shook my head numbly. Elijah was lying. If I didn't do something soon, he'd never take me to see Luke.

"No!" The word escaped my mouth before I could stop it, and Joseph's head swiveled in my direction, pleading with me not to cause a scene. "I won't meet your congregation or play your wife until you let me see him."

Hushed voices whispered through the crowd. Good. Let them see a bit of my anger. Maybe that would jolt them out of their Elijah-worshiping trance.

"Fair enough," Elijah said before turning toward the crowd. "My wife and I need some time alone. As you can imagine, this has all been quite overwhelming for her, and she needs a few moments to collect herself."

His announcement was met with a chorus of "Of course," every face smiling in acknowledgment. God, he had them all.

"If you all kindly adjourn to the community center, my wife and I will be along shortly."

I stood there next to him, his fingers wrapped tightly around mine until the last person cleared the doorway, and then gave him my demand. "I want to see him. Now."

Elijah's gentleness faded, pure rage burrowing through his eyes. He brought his hand down hard across my left cheek and I staggered backward, the sting bringing tears to my eyes.

Joseph caught me and ran his hand down my reddened face, gently wiping away my tears before easing me behind him. He glared at his father. "Don't you *ever* hit her again."

"She's *my* wife, Joseph. I'll do with her as I please, and you will not interfere."

"Please, I'm sorry," I said, trying to calm them both down for fear that Elijah would change his mind about my seeing Luke. "I'll do as you ask, always, but I want to see him first, say goodbye."

I focused all of my energy on my tone, hoping Elijah

would buy my fake apology. I didn't mean a word of it, but Elijah was a madman, and until I learned how to play his game, I was as good as dead.

TWENTY-NINE

I ended up in the same room I'd just left, but my clothes and the papers I'd been forced to memorize were gone. It was dark out now. No stars. Not even a moon to cast the slightest glow through the window.

I half expected to find Luke bound and gagged, bleeding from a crisscross of cleansing wounds. But he wasn't there, and my heart sank.

"Where is he?" I asked, wondering if I'd been played.

"Patience, Rebekah. He'll be here soon."

I took a seat on the bed and scooted back until I hit the wall. The bed dipped next to me, and I looked up and saw Joseph inching closer. His eyes were glued to my reddened cheek, his hands trembling with rage.

It was deathly quiet, none of us uttering a single word. The creak of the bedsprings as Joseph moved, the whine of the heat vent above me clicking on, and the soft rhythmic tapping of Elijah's foot against the floor put me on edge.

The door finally opened and two identical faces came into view—James and Abram—each struggling with the person they held between them. Blindfolded and bound, the person was putting up a fight, twisting and kicking as he cursed incoherently behind the gag.

I knew from the voice alone that it wasn't Luke. It was Mike.

"Oh my God!" I gasped as I stood up and quickly scanned Mike for any injuries. He looked tired and bruised and there was a patch of dried blood on the corner of his mouth. But he was fighting hard, and that meant he was still strong.

The excitement of seeing Mike quickly faded, leaving behind anger. "You promised me Luke!"

Elijah vacated his seat and motioned to his nephews to drop Mike there. "I promised you could see your friend. I never said which one."

I could've killed Elijah right there—the hell with my life, with Mike's and Luke's—had Joseph not stopped me. His hands circled around my waist, my feet leaving the floor as he spun me around and crushed my body to his chest.

"Don't," Joseph whispered into my ear, his arms squeezing me in place as I tried to wiggle free. "Stop fighting me, stop fighting him and calm down."

Behind those words was a reminder that I needed to play along so we could get Elijah out of the room. I'd try. For Mike or Luke...for Eden, I'd try. "Okay," I said, and

Joseph put me down, keeping his arm around my waist in case I lost it again.

Elijah ignored us. He was too busy circling Mike, as if trying deciding which part of him to mangle. He stopped directly behind him, removed the blindfold, and then ran his hand across his throat, yanking Mike's head back. "Of course, if she doesn't want you, I'd be happy to toss you back in with your brother."

Panic exploded through Mike, his entire body starting to shake. Wherever Elijah had stashed them, it wasn't good.

Slowly, so as not to alarm Joseph, I stepped forward. "No. I want him," I said. "I assumed you were bringing Luke. My mistake, not yours."

"I don't make mistakes," Elijah said.

He let go of Mike's head, and Mike winced as his chin fell forward. I did a quick scan of his hands, counted all ten of his fingers before moving to his arms and legs. I couldn't see any obvious injuries, but after being sliced open three times in the name of God, I knew Mike could have any number of wounds hidden beneath his clothes.

"Lucky for you, my new wife isn't picky."

Mike's eyes flashed wide at Elijah's declaration. Apparently he hadn't been told about my new status in the community.

"Take the gag off. I want to talk to him. Please." It took an enormous amount of effort to add that last word. To beg Elijah for anything made me feel sick, like I'd given in. But at that point I would've begged, pleaded, traded my own life if it meant saving Mike and Luke's.

"I'll do you one better. Being that it is our wedding night and your egocentric customs dictate I present you with a gift, I'll make *him* your gift. I'll give you an hour with him. Joseph will stay with you. Consider him a chaperone of sorts."

There was no way Elijah trusted either of us that much. The man I knew wasn't generous or trusting or even empathetic. He was calculated and manipulative. Deadly. Which meant the time he was gifting me with Mike would come with a price.

"What's the catch?" I asked.

"No catch. Rather, some added insurance." Elijah walked over to his nephews and wedged himself in between them. "I could use your boyfriend, Luke, but he's more useful to me alive than dead. You know ... the whole *one-indiscretion-one-finger* bargain we agreed upon."

He paused and looked from James to Abram, then back to me. The obvious pleasure in his voice had me searching out Joseph, desperately hoping he could give me some silent insight into what dark, twisted path his father's mind was traveling down now.

Elijah caught my look and said, "Even my son can't save you from this one."

"What are you talking about?" I yelled. I was tired of his cryptic messages. I didn't have the energy to decipher his insane mind and plan my own escape at the same time.

Elijah spread his arms, each one circling around the shoulders of Abram and James. "The way I see it, both are completely disposable to me. They have a habit of swaying from the righteous course, and for that, I fear, they will never flourish in Purity Springs. It's only a matter of time before they succumb to the evils of the outside world, forcing me to do what is necessary rather than risk my entire community. To me, which one goes first doesn't matter. You choose."

"Choose?" My eyes darted between the twins as I struggled to understand what Elijah was saying. "Choose what?"

"I'm going to give you an hour with your friend, and then I'm going to return. If you aren't here, if that boy is not standing right here, exactly where I left him, then one of them dies. Which one is up to you."

Was he kidding me? How was I supposed to choose? They were only fourteen, and I knew nothing about them. And they were twins. Identical twins. I couldn't even tell them apart. Did he honestly expect me to casually pick one to die?

"Time's a-wasting." Elijah flicked his hand to see his watch, the motion wrenching one of boy's necks painfully close. "I'm thinking your sixty minutes starts right— about—now."

I turned toward Joseph, praying he had some sort of contingency plan. He shook his head and whispered, "Pick one."

Holy crap, he was serious. They were both serious. Looking up, I did my best to avoid making eye contact with either boy. Their expressions were blank, their posture steady and straight, but I could feel the fear pouring off them, could taste the bitter scent of it in the air.

My gaze must've landed on the one to left for a fraction of a second too long, and the decision was made. "James it is," Elijah said and moved toward the door. "Fear not, boys, so long as my wife makes the right decision, neither of you will be harmed. *Yet.*" He said that last part under his breath, a quiet acknowledgment of the fact that they wouldn't be safe forever.

"And Joseph," Elijah said, not bothering to turn around as he opened the door, "I knew you were planning on running with your mother. Consider this a test, your last chance to prove where your loyalty truly lies. It shouldn't be hard, son, but consider your cousin James a little added incentive to make sure you act wisely."

They filed out of the room. James turned back once, his haunted gaze landing squarely on me. I wanted to reach out to him, to tell him it'd be okay, but I couldn't move. I could barely think.

"Will he... Will he..." I couldn't get the words out, couldn't wrap my head around the idea that Elijah would actually kill his own nephew as a warning to me.

"My father wants to see if I'll choose you over them... over my own family," Joseph said. "He's testing me, Dee, not you. He won't give you up no matter what."

I shook my head, not understanding what he was saying.

"Remember how he said he needed a son, one who would carry on the prophecy?" I nodded, and Joseph continued. "I'm it. Well, at least until..."

The weight of his words strangled me. If I left, if I grabbed Mike and ran, then James would die. And if Joseph did nothing to stop me, then he was as good as dead too.

THIRTY

An hour was a long time when I was stuck in physics class or serving out detention. But here, trapped in a world controlled by Elijah Hawkins, sixty minutes wasn't nearly long enough.

I had the gag out of Mike's mouth and was furiously working on the restraints that bound his hands behind his back. Joseph came around to help, struggling against Mike's clenching fists to loosen the ties.

The minute he was free, Mike let his fist fly straight into Joseph's jaw. I didn't try to stop him. Hell, I'd wanted to do that myself when I first woke up. I'd only held off because Joseph was all I had.

Mike paused for only a second—long enough to see the blood soaking through my bandages—before he grabbed

Joseph again. He hauled him up off the floor and pinned him to the wall.

"First, you're going to tell me exactly where that man has stashed my brother, and then I'm gonna kill you."

Mike's hand circled Joseph's throat, the pressure making speech impossible. "Mike, stop! STOP!" I screamed. Joseph's face was bright red, his eyes tearing up as he struggled to breath. "You're killing him!"

Mike loosened his grip and leveled a hate-fueled glare in my direction. "Damn straight I am," he yelled as he gave Joseph another hard shove into the wall. "Give me one good reason why I should let him live?"

Somehow, Joseph had managed to wedge his hand between himself and Mike. He shoved Mike away and coughed, gasping to fill his lungs. "Because I'm the one trying to save you guys, that's why."

"Oh that's great. *You're* trying to save us? The guy who used his friends to kidnap us in the first place is suddenly on our side?" Mike fired back.

"That's not what I intended—"

"You think I give a shit what you intended?" Mike cut in, his anger flaring. "All I know is that you left us both for dead and took Dee. I don't care about saving your sister, and I don't care if he kills that James kid. All I'm gonna do is take Dee, find Luke, and get the hell out of here."

Mike looked at me, his expression hard and determined as he held out his hand for me to take. "Let's go."

I reached out and grabbed Mike's hand, cringing as my fingers skirted over a patch of dried blood. I didn't know if it was a "cleansing" wound or a gash from him trying to claw his way out of the zip-ties Elijah had tightened around his wrists, but I knew that when we got out of here, *if* we got out of here, I'd ask exactly what Elijah had done to them.

"We need his help," I whispered, praying that my instincts weren't wrong. Joseph was on our side. Joseph was, in fact, the one person we could trust on the inside. "We'll never get out of here without his help."

Mike sighed, his hand squeezing mine with excruciating force. "Help? *Help?* Are you insane, Dee? How has he helped us so far?"

I didn't know how to answer that. It wasn't something I could explain, more of an overwhelming feeling that had it not been for Joseph, I would've been dead by now. Plus, I knew Joseph wanted out of here as bad as me. I'd recognized the desperation radiating off him the second we met. I knew the look—the one that said no matter what it cost you, you'd survive—because I wore it myself. It wasn't Joseph I trusted, it was that look.

"Have you seen yourself, Dee? You're pale and your arms are covered in blood."

Mike squatted down in front of me, studying me as if he was searching for some sort of truth. My guess was he wanted to know if I was starting to believe all the crap they were spewing in this town.

"You realize you're defending the kid who sold you out, right?" Mike asked. "The one who dragged you in here and left me and Luke for dead."

I knew who I was defending, and no, I wasn't buying

what Elijah was selling. And as for Luke, I was pretty sure that was all Elijah's doing.

"Look at me," Mike said as he grabbed my chin. "The last thing I saw, the last thing *Luke* saw, was this kid dragging you away. How can you believe anything he says?"

I dropped my gaze to the floor. I knew Joseph had gotten me hurt. He'd hauled me into this hellhole on the ridiculous notion that I was strong enough to save his sister. But looking at him now, I felt different. I didn't merely *see* the myriad of scars on his body or the pain in his eyes, I *understood* them. There was no going back from that, no erasing the knowledge that had already been burned into my soul and carved into my arms.

"I know," I whispered. "But you have no idea what's going to happen to them. I won't leave Joseph here. I won't let Elijah hurt those two boys or Eden. Not if there's a chance we can get them out."

Mike cocked his head as if staring at a stranger. "What are you saying? This kid is seven shades of crazy, Dee, and you want to save him? Keep him around?"

I was fully aware Mike thought I'd lost it. Maybe I had. "I'm saying I want to find Luke and get out of here. But I want to take them with us."

With a grunt of disgust, Mike gave up trying to reason with me and turned to Joseph. "What did you do to her? What is this, some kind of brainwashing or drugs or something?"

"You don't—" I went to explain, but Mike cut me off.

"Forget it," Mike said. "I don't care what he did or what

he said to make you *think* you need to save him. It doesn't matter, because I'm not giving you a choice. I'm leaving and taking you with me."

He moved to pick me up, to physically remove me from this place, but Joseph shoved him away.

Mike growled and squared off. "Are you kidding me? You honestly think you need to protect Dee from *me*? Newsflash, kid, you're the problem here, not me. But if you're looking for a fight, I'm game." He widened his stance and grinned, curling his fingers, inviting Joseph to take his best shot.

Joseph did exactly that. He straightened up and pulled his fist back. I grabbed onto his arm before he could swing. Joseph may have been big, but Mike was pissed off. Either way, this wasn't going to end well.

"Let it go, Joseph. This is—"

I tried to ease them down, but Joseph shook me off. "I didn't do anything to her. I've been doing my best to keep her safe, to protect her from my father since we got here. Not once have I touched her. Not once!"

Mike cast a suspicious glare my way, and I nodded. It was true. Joseph's mind was broken and worked in a completely different way than ours, but he'd kept his word. He'd even taken a beating to protect us. In his own delusional way, Joseph had kept me safe.

I headed for the door. Mike and Joseph could stay here all night locked in their pissing match for all I cared. I was going to find Luke.

"Do you have any clue where Luke might be?" I asked Mike.

"No. We were locked in that damn sin shack for a few hours, but then that man —"

"Elijah," I interrupted.

"Whatever," Mike said, obviously irritated that the crazy man and I were on a first-name basis. "His father split us up this morning, put me in a separate room from Luke. I was blindfolded the entire way, so I have no idea what building we were in, but it was a good ten-minute walk at least."

I dropped my head to my hands, frustrated and scared by the very real possibility that we would never find Luke.

"I could hear him, though," Mike added quickly. "Every once in a while I'd hear his voice, so I know he was close. We were probably only a room apart."

"You could hear Luke?" I asked. "Like, you heard him talking to Elijah?"

Mike shifted his gaze to the ground so I couldn't read his expression. "No, not all the time, and he never seemed to hear me. But there was…" He trailed off, his hands hanging limply at his sides.

"Was what?" I asked.

"Screaming."

The word was choked, Mike's voice cracking as if uttering that one word was excruciatingly painful.

I inhaled sharply, wishing more than anything I could erase everything I'd just heard. Luke was tucked away in some torture chamber and I was sitting here, wasting time as Mike and I fought over Joseph.

I fisted Joseph's shirt in my hands and shook him hard. "Where is he? Where would your father hide him?"

Joseph shrugged, his focus scattered as if he was searching his mind for a hidden clue as to where Luke was.

I let go of his shirt and did my best to soften my tone. "Where is Luke? Think, Joseph. Where?"

Joseph took a step toward Mike and spoke. "The place you were in ... do you remember anything about it?"

Mike shook his head. "Not much. Like I said, thanks to that asshole father of yours, I was blindfolded the whole time and tied down."

"Chair or floor?" Joseph asked.

"Neither," Mike answered quickly. "It was a bed."

Without a moment's pause, Joseph rattled off his next question: "Twin or full?"

"Small. Twin, I guess," Mike replied. "Why?"

Joseph ignored his question and followed up with one of his own. It was as if he already knew where his father had stashed Luke, and every question, every answer, confirmed his suspicion. "Do you remember what it smelled like?"

"I don't know, earthy? Maybe a little sweet. Like a combination of burnt paper and pot."

I swung my head toward Joseph, doubtful that anyone in this town knew what pot was, never mind had smoked it. Joseph caught my look of confusion and brushed it off, heading for the door. "I know exactly where he is. Let's go."

THIRTY-ONE

I found myself staring at the house we'd crashed in twenty-four hours ago. Elijah had brought Luke home. That crazy son-of-a-bitch was holding my boyfriend in his own house.

"You sure?" Mike asked, his gaze flickering anxiously over the darkened front window.

"Positive. There's a room in our basement. My father used to lock me in it all the time," Joseph said, a shiver working its way through his body. "He'd say that the only way to rid my mind of childhood fantasies was to surround myself in complete stillness."

I could only guess what childhood fantasies would warrant such a punishment. Perhaps pretending a block of wood was a truck or dreaming about being a pirate. Or better yet, making Eden a doll.

"It's small, dark, and completely soundproof," Joseph

continued. "You wouldn't have heard him unless my father opened the door."

Mike opened the front door to the house and the smell hit me, hard and strong. When we let ourselves in last night, all I'd registered was burnt pasta and garlic. Mike had pinned it right; it now reeked of burnt paper and weed.

"What's that smell?" I asked.

"Sage," Joseph responded. "My father burns it to rid the house of evil. He's the only one who can do it, the only person *pure* enough to perform such a ritual. When my uncles come home for a visit, he does the same there, cleanses them and their houses so whatever they may have brought with them from the outside doesn't infect the rest of us."

Mike crossed the threshold, his bloody knuckles tensing into fists. It was silent, and we turned to each other, our ears straining to pick up the slightest noise. We got nothing, forcing Mike to ask, "Where is he?"

"There's an old bookshelf in the basement. Next to it is a door," Joseph said. "It's locked. It's always locked, but my guess is Luke's in there."

Mike held out his hand. "Key."

"Top shelf, underneath the Bible," Joseph said, and I prayed that the key was still there, that Elijah hadn't slipped it into his pocket when he'd left to bring me Luke's finger.

The basement staircase was at the far end of the kitchen. It doubled as a utility closet, several mops and a dustpan hanging from hooks on the wall. I remembered the high-pitched squeak of the door when we opened it last night, when Luke and Mike made their way down to see if the family who lived here was camped out in some sort of storm shelter. I'd found the sound eerie then. Now it was worse.

I hit the switch and light flooded the room. Yesterday, storage boxes had lined the cement walls of the basement. Now the one being stored down there was Luke.

"There," Joseph said, extending a hand to his left.

I went for the bookcase. It was too high, and I had to stand up on the bottom ledge in order to reach the top shelf. Even then I couldn't see the key. I blindly swiped the Bible away, searching for the key. My fingers barely grazed a cold piece of metal and I circled back, grabbing onto the tiny thing like it was my lifeline. In a way, it was.

The door was right where Joseph said it would be. "You remember seeing that door last night?" I asked Mike, hoping to God I wasn't losing my mind.

"Yup. Luke tried it, but it was locked. We figured it was a cedar closet or something filled with valuables."

I had the key in the lock, my hand shaking and frozen in place. Luke was the strongest person I knew, the one person who I could always count on to make things better. If he was hurt, if the survival of all of us landed solely on *my* shoulders, then I was dead. We all were.

"I got it," Mike said, his hand covering mine.

I looked up, and he nodded but didn't try for words. He couldn't. He was probably wrestling with the same fears as me.

Backing up, I gave Mike full access to the door, to the lock, to his brother on the other side. He turned the key and the lock clicked open, the sound echoing off the walls.

I expected Mike to slam the door open and run headlong into that room. He didn't. He froze like me.

"Let's get one thing straight," Mike said. "I don't care who that James kid is, or whether or not Elijah actually plans to kill him. I'm not going back into that town, and neither is Dee. Whatever it takes, *whoever* it takes to get us out of here is what I'm going to do. You get in my way, Joseph, and I'll kill you myself."

THIRTY-TWO

Mike eased the door open as if he was scared of what he'd find on the other side. I was with him on that. With my luck, Elijah would be sitting there waiting for us, bone-saw in hand. I shook off that thought and pushed past Mike. By this point, I didn't care what or who lurked behind that door. I wanted Luke.

The smell hit me first, stale and rancid. It was dead silent—the sound of my own footsteps on the cement floor was the only noise—and pitch dark. I stumbled around blindly, searching for the light switch.

"Luke?"

I waited for a response, for anything that would indicate we'd come to the right place. No sound, not even a whimper to tell me which direction to turn.

I purposefully shut my mind down and refused to process the smells, the silence, everything my brain was trying to force onto me. Luke was fine. He'd been stuck down here with no windows. No ventilation. No bathroom. Of course it was going to stink, but he—was—fine.

"I need a light," I yelled.

"There isn't one," Joseph said as he stepped inside and adjusted the tiny flame of a lantern. "This place was intended to be quiet and completely dark so you'd have nothing but your conscience to distract you."

The lantern flared to life, coating the walls in an orange glow. I followed the light as he swung it from one wall to the next, hoping that it would land on Luke.

The light flashed over something solid in the middle of the room. I grabbed the lantern from Joseph and ran toward it. My feet slid out from underneath me, and I fell to my knees on the wet ground. Both my palms hit the floor and I lost control of the lantern. The light flickered twice before it steadied. Warmth seeped through my skirt, and a dark stain seeped through the stark white fabric as a rusty metallic smell filled my nose.

My body stiffened in recognition. I knew what it was— that dense, dark liquid that was now coating most of my lower body. I put my hands down anyway, flattening them against the floor and into the moisture. They came up red. Bright red and dripping. It was wet, not sticky or dried. I grabbed onto that knowledge and forced myself to lift my head. Then I screamed.

"Mike!"

He was there in an instant, pushing me out of the way as he tore at the restraints that bound Luke's feet to the chair.

"I need more light," he yelled, and I held out the lantern, my arm brushing Luke's leg. It was cold and stiff. I squeezed his calf and waited for his muscle to twitch. Nothing. I dug my nails into his thigh, thinking a bit of pain would bring him around, awaken him from whatever sleep he was in.

"He's not moving," I choked out. "Mike, do something. He's not moving."

"I know. Help me get him untied."

Mike had Luke's feet free and was frantically working on his arms. They were stretched back and bound so tight that I wondered if his shoulders were dislocated or his muscles torn.

I squatted down next to Mike to help, but my hands were shaking so badly that I couldn't maneuver the rope. Tears streamed down my cheeks and my entire body convulsed with terror, anger, and remorse.

"Dee, let me," Joseph said as he took my hand in his. He wrapped my fingers around the handle of a second lantern and gently pushed me aside before taking my spot and manipulating the knots himself.

"Luke?" I whispered. Through the shadows, I could see that his eyes were open. His head was slung forward, his jaw slack.

"Luke?" I said again.

The panic slowly welled in my soul, and I reached out to touch his face. My hand molded to his cheek, a day's worth of stubble rubbing against my palm. Even that couldn't drive away the coldness of his skin.

They say that the dead look peaceful and relaxed, as if they've passed onto a better place. But that's not what I saw when I looked at Luke. What I saw was agony. Pure, unadulterated agony.

The ropes finally gave way and Luke slumped forward, his entire body falling into my lap. I struggled under his weight and ended up in the stale pool of blood, Luke cradled in my arms.

He wasn't wearing a shirt, and for a brief second I let myself believe that's why he was so cold. The cellar was damp and unheated. If I warmed him up, if I could get his body to accept my heat, then he'd be fine.

"It's okay, baby," I cried as I held him to me, rocking him and willing my strength, my very essence, into him. "I'm going to take you home. It's all going to be fine."

I wrapped my arm around his waist, anchoring him to me, while my free hand searched for a pulse. I silently pleaded, would've gladly bartered away my own life for one small movement of his chest, one tiny tick of a pulse. Even a gasp of pain would've been welcomed.

There was blood, so much blood. I could barely find the spot beneath his jaw I was looking for. I settled my finger there and held my breath as I waited for the faint beat of life.

"Oh God." I tried again, my fingers slipping to the other side of his neck as I hoped beyond reason for something I knew wasn't there.

I gave up trying to find a pulse on his neck and reached for his wrist. I'd watched Luke take his own pulse a thousand times. Always on the wrist, always the same spot.

A hand on my shoulder stopped me, and I twitched, jerking off whoever it was. I could do this. I could prove Luke wasn't gone. The hand came back and latched on so hard that I had no choice but to turn and look.

"Dee," Mike said. "Let me see him."

"No," I cried out. I wasn't letting anybody have him. *Anybody.*

"Dee, let go. Please, God, let me see him."

Mike's voice cracked, and I looked up, saw the sheen of tears threatening to overwhelm him. I shook my head and held on tighter. Luke wasn't dead. There was no reason for Mike to lose it. No reason for the tears slipping down his face. Luke wasn't gone. He wasn't. I wouldn't let him be.

"Let go!" Mike screamed, prying Luke from my arms. I went at him, intent on getting Luke back. I needed Luke! I needed to feel him against me. Luke was mine. He belonged to me.

Joseph caught me around the waist and pulled me into his chest. I turned my anger on him, hurling every foul word I could think of at him, but he simply held me tighter, whispering for me to calm down.

Mike sat down and leaned Luke against his own chest, then put his ear to Luke's mouth in search of a breath. He hovered over him for what seemed like an eternity. Slowly, his hand slid to Luke's chest, vainly seeking the muted thump of his heart, the expansion of his lungs ... something, anything, that would indicate that we had time.

Mike finally shook his head, his face pale as the tears poured from his eyes. Like I'd done, he gathered Luke up in his arms and rocked him, quietly swearing against all that was sacred and holy to kill the person who did this.

"No. *NO!*" I thrashed in Joseph's arms, kicked at his legs as the gut-wrenching realization hit me. Luke was gone. My boyfriend. My life. My everything. Gone.

One good kick to the shin and Joseph let me go. I fell to the ground and crawled to Luke. I went to take him, to pull him into my arms, but Mike wouldn't let him go. He pushed me away with the heel of his foot and dragged Luke farther into his arms, buried his head in his brother's neck and sobbed.

I slammed my fists into the ground and screamed. The pain searing through my hands and knuckles was barely enough to keep me conscious, to keep what little sanity I had left from slipping away completely. I pulled myself up and covered my ears to drown out Mike's cries. It didn't work. His guttural pleas bounced off the cold walls, piercing my soul. It wasn't supposed to be this way. It. Wasn't. Supposed. To. Be. This. Way.

I went for the only thing I could reach—the lantern—and threw it at the wall. Small pieces of glass rained down to the floor, but that didn't help. The rage inside me was building, drowning me, and I went for the chair.

It was bolted to the ground, but I yanked anyway, throwing all my energy into ripping it from its anchors. I screamed and tugged again, the force jerking me forward and straight into Joseph's arms. I pushed at him, would've thrown him through the wall if I could've.

"Stop, Dee. Please, stop," Joseph said as he pulled me

into his chest again and folded his arms securely around me. "I promise it's going to be okay."

He kept chanting those words as if his assurances were what I needed. They weren't; the only thing I'd ever needed was lying there dead.

"It's not okay," I sobbed as I turned my head to the side and looked down at Luke. "It's never going to be okay again."

Luke's body lay limp in Mike's arms, his struggle clearly visible in the wounds defiling his skin. I knew exactly what the three-inch slits lining his body were. Elijah had bled Luke with no restraint or regard. I had seven wounds on my arms. Three on the right and four on the left. But Luke was covered in them. His arms were a mess of crisscross patterns, his chest marred and soaked in blood. His hair had been cut so short that parts of his scalp were visible. His shoes were gone, his skin red and broken where he'd struggled against his restraints.

I focused on the thin red lines around his wrist, memorized them rather than look at his hands and confirm what I knew to me true. With one deep breath, I looked down and gasped. His middle finger was gone, a clean white bandage covering the wound. His whole hand was clean, not a mark or scrap of dirt on it.

I reached out and unwound that bandage, several inches of gauze falling to the floor. I ran my finger across the palm of his hand. It was exactly like I remembered—soft and calloused at the same time. I let my hand play down each one of his intact fingers before stopping and looking at what was missing.

I couldn't believe what I was seeing. That son of a bitch had taken off Luke's finger, then had the insane decency to stitch the wound closed. Why bother? Why the hell would you bother to patch him up if you only intended to let him die?

He was insane. Elijah Hawkins wasn't a religious zealot; he was completely crazy. And crazy wasn't something you could reason with.

THIRTY-THREE

The silence was agonizing. Each breath I managed to take ached, burning my lungs as I struggled to process the truth. Nothing, not years of enduring my father's abuse, not even the vague knowledge that I might be bound to Elijah Hawkins forever, compared to the soul-crushing pain I was feeling.

I tried to stand but dizziness took over, the floor pitching and rocking beneath me. I didn't reach out to Joseph or Mike to steady myself. With my world crashing down around me, I honestly didn't care if I fell. I didn't care if I died. In fact, death would've been welcomed.

"This can't be happening. This can't be happening," I said over and over, my own voice sounding hollow and foreign.

Joseph dropped to the floor next to me. His hand shook as it ran over my back, and I shrugged him off. I didn't want to be touched or moved. I needed to stay right where I was, my hands locked around my knees as I stared into Luke's dead eyes. If I let go, if I moved even an inch, then I'd lose every part of me.

No, I needed to stay like this, physically—literally—holding myself together.

Mike started crying again, his broken sobs filling the room with a horrible, empty sound. I shuddered and huddled farther into myself as I watched him through the sheen of my own tears, totally unable to say or do anything to make it better.

"We need to go," Joseph said.

Mike lifted Luke from his lap and eased him against the wall. Even in the dark, I could see the pain in Mike's eyes, his despair taking hold. He ran the back of his sleeve across his face before bending down and whispering to his brother, "He'll pay for this. If it's the last thing I ever do, I'll make sure he pays."

"You ready to go?" Joseph asked.

"Go? Go where? Luke is dead!"

"I know, Dee, and I'm sorry. I truly am. I never expected my father to . . . " Joseph trailed off as he quickly looked at his watch. "It's been nearly an hour since my father left us in that room. We have to go. Now."

"I'm not going anywhere. Not without Luke," I said.

Joseph let out a frustrated sigh and turned to Mike. They could team up on me for all I cared. Dead or not, I wasn't leaving Luke here alone.

"Listen, Dee," Mike said, pausing to clear the tears from his throat. "Joseph is right. We gotta go."

"No." It was one word, but it held more conviction than anything I'd ever said.

Mike closed the short distance between us and put his hands on either side of my face. Streams of tears ran down his face, and his hands trembled against my cheeks as he took in another ragged breath. Somehow I'd forgotten that Luke wasn't only my rock; he was Mike's too.

"We can't do anything for Luke," Mike said. "But I can save you. He made me swear to get you out of here. I promised him that if I got the chance, I'd forget about saving him and go find you."

I didn't care about Mike's stupid promise; I wasn't leaving Luke. "No. I won't go."

I looked around the dank room, pausing on the details I hadn't noticed when we came in. The piles of vomit. The heap of blood-soaked rags lying in the corner. One of Luke's sneakers, stained red in the shadows. This was how Luke had died—alone and in the basement of a narcissist with nothing but darkness and squalor to keep him company. He didn't deserve this. Nobody deserved this.

I'd thought I was helping him. I'd believed that submitting to Elijah's insanity would protect Luke. What an absolute idiot I'd been.

"You have no idea what that man will do to him," I said. Elijah would probably find some twisted way to offer Luke's body up as a sacrifice to God...to himself. "We can't leave him here, Mike. We can't."

The second Mike looked down at Luke, I knew he'd

sided with me. "Fine. We'll take him with us. We'll bring him home."

"We won't get half a mile outside of town carrying him," Joseph argued.

"Half a mile? You won't get *five feet* up those steps without him," Mike replied, his hand sweeping out in my direction. "Trust me. I know Dee better than you ever will, and she's not leaving without him. And I'm not leaving without her." He sidestepped around Joseph and held his hand out for me to take. "I'll carry him home, Dee."

I took Mike's hand. The heat of tears warmed my face again and Mike buried me in his chest, hugging me so tight I could feel his heart beating against my cheek. His shoulders shook as the strength he'd tried so hard to gather cracked and fell away.

A shuffling sound from behind me caught my attention, and I glanced up and realized Luke was gone. Joseph had him slung over his shoulder and was making his way toward the stairs.

Mike followed my gaze, his whole body vibrating with anger. "Take your hands off him," Mike said as he tore Luke from Joseph's arms. "I don't need your help carrying him."

"I never would've brought Dee here, any of you here, if I'd known this would happen," Joseph said.

Tears still rimmed Mike's eyes and I looked away, desperate to allow him that tiny shred of dignity as he gently settled his only brother over his shoulder. He was taking Luke home; we both needed to take Luke home.

THIRTY-FOUR

I flung open the front door and a momentary sense of peace filled me as I breathed in the night air. Finally, I was able to rid my senses of the horrible stench of the basement.

The streetlights cast a strange, iridescent light over the yard, doing little to keep the darkness at bay. If you'd asked me before, I would've told you I was afraid of the dark and embarrassingly pointed to the nightlight Mrs. Hooper kept in the upstairs hall. Not anymore. Now the darkness kept us hidden, gave us a shot at escaping unnoticed.

We decided to let Joseph lead, figuring he would know the quickest route to safety. Our goal wasn't to make it home in one night, just to get safely out of Elijah's striking distance.

I felt more than saw Elijah emerge from the shadows, and with one deep breath, I turned around to face him.

"Going somewhere, Rebekah?"

Joseph and Mike slowly turned around at the sound of his voice. Mike's hand flexed, the rage he'd tamped down flying full throttle to the surface.

I thought about taking off, just running as fast as I could in the opposite direction, and if it hadn't been for what Elijah was holding in front of him, I probably would've. Elijah had James by the throat, kicking at the back of the boy's feet to make him walk. James was pale and sweating, but he wasn't lashing out or trying to break free. It wasn't until I saw the glint of the blade at James's neck that I figured out why.

James silently begged me to help him, the plea encased in tears that nearly brought me to my knees. I couldn't help him. I was unarmed, Mike was loaded down with Luke, and Joseph looked as scared his cousin. That crazy old man had us stuck, unsure of what to do or where to run.

"James," I muttered, hoping he'd hear the apology in my tone.

Elijah wrenched James's neck back farther, the knife poised at his skin like a promise. "I see you found your brother," he said to Mike, his gaze skimming over Luke's body. "I tried, you know. I begged him to give up his contemptuous ways. But unlike you, he wouldn't acknowledge my divinity. He kept damning me to hell, all in the name of *her*."

Elijah's words sunk in, left me standing there with nothing but the horrid truth ringing in my ears. Luke had been fighting for me, had spent his last hours cursing Elijah until it got him killed.

"There is no point in taking him home," Elijah continued. "Even a Christian burial won't save his soul."

Elijah repositioned the knife, twisting it to elicit a gasp from James's lips. "It's actually better this way. Somebody as tainted as Luke needed to be released from the confines of this world and returned to his maker."

I shrieked, a sound so intense and full of anger that I lost the ability to think. I wanted to tear every scrap of skin from Elijah's body and stand over him as he took his last breath.

"Don't," Joseph whispered, anticipating my actions. "You go after him and he'll kill James. Please, Dee, don't give him a reason. Father," he said, turning to Elijah with a plea in his voice, a plea I knew would go unanswered, "let them go. I'll stay. I'll submit to whatever you deem necessary, but please, let them go."

"The thought of you leaving never crossed my mind, son. You were born and raised here, taught in our ways. And here is where you will die."

Maybe that was Elijah's endgame. Maybe he truly wanted to see us all dead, including his own son.

"What do you want from us?" Mike's voice came from behind me. I turned and found myself staring at Luke's thighs. They were covered in blood and whatever other horrible, sickening liquid had begun to seep from his body.

"That's the wrong question." Elijah stepped closer, dragging James with him. "You entrusted me with your soul, boy, agreed to go through the cleansing ritual and join our humble community. I expect you to keep your word."

"I don't owe you shit," Mike fired back. "Like you said,

I'm the smart one here. I said everything you wanted to hear, and what do you know? Here I am, alive and well."

"For now," Elijah said, smiling. He swung James around to face me, pushing him forward so that our feet touched and our breath mingled. "About your little indiscretion, Rebekah."

I saw one thing and one thing only... the knife, clean and sharp.

"I believe I made myself quite clear when I left, did I not?" Elijah asked.

I opened my mouth, had to shut it and swallow hard twice before I came out with, "Please." Not *I'll do what you want* or *take me instead*. All I could manage was a weak, feeble "please."

"Forgiveness is something I will grant you, because I understand the world you have lived in. I know that it will take great courage and strength on my part to keep you pure," Elijah said. "But forgiveness by no means clears you of guilt, and for that you must pay a separate price of redemption."

"Me!" I screamed, finally finding the courage to offer myself up. "Not him. I was the one who left to find Luke. I was the one who ran from you. Not James."

"Trust me in this," Elijah said. "This is a punishment you will not soon forget."

He turned to James and laid the gentlest of kisses on the side of his head. "By all that is holy, I release you from the confines of this world."

THIRTY-FIVE

The blade pierced James's pale skin. His body went rigid in fear and Elijah paused, sinking the knife deeper until more and more of the gleaming silver disappeared and the first hint of blood trickled out.

James gasped as Elijah pulled back, pausing long enough to smile at me before sinking the sharp edge fully into the boy's throat. With one fluid motion, Elijah swept the knife straight across, leaving behind a gaping red smile in James's neck.

Clutching at his throat, James fell to his knees. His lips parted in a silent scream as his startled gaze met mine, fear eclipsing his pain. The blood pulsed out in rhythmic intervals, each spurt hanging in the air for what felt like an eternity before raining to the ground in a hideous red trail.

The puddle of red grew from three feet to five, spreading out until my clogs were bathed in it. I counted five spurts before he gurgled, as if choking on his own blood.

James reached out for me, one hand latching on to the bottom of my skirt. I jumped back and collided with Mike. The force of my movement sent us both tumbling backward, Mike struggling under Luke's weight and me scrambling to get as far away from James's panicked stare as possible.

I landed on my butt, Mike and Luke splayed out next to me on the road. Joseph grabbed both my shoulders and pulled me up, his hands shaking as he tucked me into his shoulder. Mike jumped to his feet next to us, then crouched down like he was preparing to attack. He reminded me of Luke, the determined look, the rigid set of his shoulders not so different from Luke's stance on the defensive line. Except this wasn't a two-hundred-pound offensive guard from Long Island. This was an insane man with a God-complex wielding a knife.

"Mike, don't."

He ignored me, dropped his head, and surged forward, hitting Elijah's body with such force that the knife flew through the air. It hit the pavement, the clash of the metal against the road thundering through the darkness.

I circled behind them looking for the knife, begging the moon to appear long enough for me to find it. The sound of a fist hitting bone echoed through the clear air. All I could make out were two hazy figures locked in battle, and I wondered if it was Elijah's jaw or Mike's knuckles taking most of the damage.

The clouds shifted, and I finally caught a glimpse of Elijah. His head was tilted back against the pavement as he took Mike's next blow. I watched in disbelief as Elijah's hand shot out to his left, the blade I was searching for now lodged in his hand.

"Joseph!" I screamed.

I sprinted forward when Joseph didn't move, pissed that he was staring into the distance rather than helping me. Helping Mike.

A hint of laughter escaped Elijah's lips as his fingers tensed around the hilt of the knife. Mike pulled his hand back, his entire body trembling with rage. He let his fist fly, and that's when Elijah struck, drove the knife upward, sinking it hilt-deep into Mike's shoulder. Mike never saw it coming; he was too focused on pummeling Elijah into the ground to notice the danger.

I caught Mike's body as he fell. His fingers wrapped around the blade protruding from his shoulder. He tensed, releasing his grip on the knife, then grabbed it again. I knew what he was preparing to do, knew it was going to hurt more coming out than it did going in.

I tried to drag Mike away from Elijah, but he dug his heels into the ground, forcing me to stop. He ground his teeth shut and pulled, wincing as the blade slowly emerged from his skin, red and gleaming sharp. Gasping, Mike doubled over and struggled to catch his breath, never once letting go of the knife he now held in his hand.

I heard frantic whispering behind me and spun around in time to see what had Joseph paralyzed. Eden was at the edge of the field, her face ashen. Beside her, Abram stood clutching his own throat as he stared at his twin brother's body splayed out on the road. Abram was in shock, his body too still, too silent in the midst of the chaos unfolding around us.

"Joseph help me," I yelled. I didn't have time for Eden's fear or Abram's pain. I needed to get Mike out of here. I needed to get us out of here.

Joseph suddenly snapped into motion, running over to me and Mike. "Keep pressure on it," he said sharply as he pushed me aside and ripped open Mike's shirt.

I nodded numbly, torn between helping Mike and keeping an eye on Elijah, who was struggling to get up. Elijah may have been hurt, but I wasn't naïve enough to think we were safe. Part of me swore that the evil coursing through his veins had some superhuman origins, one derived not from God but from the devil himself. I knew Elijah would get up. No matter how hurt, no matter how illogical it seemed, Elijah Hawkins would get up.

"Take this," I said as I tore a strip of fabric off the bottom of my skirt and handed it to Joseph. It was covered in dirt and blood—both Luke's and James's—but it was all I had

Joseph tied it around Mike's shoulder, lifting him slightly to get a tighter fit, then yanked so hard that the fabric tore. He looped it around again and tied it off.

Mike moaned under the pressure and slammed his eyes shut as he cursed Elijah. "I'm going to kill you. I swear to God, I am going to kill you!"

Footsteps echoed against the pavement. The stride was even, slow, and methodical. I counted those steps the same way I counted the spurts of James's blood, waiting for the inevitable and powerless to stop it.

Abram continued his advance, his movements that of a sleepwalking man. He stopped mere inches from us, then reached out and yanked the knife from Mike's grip. His hand trembled as he turned it over and over, his brother's and Mike's blood now coating his fingers.

Panic overwhelmed me as Abram made his way toward Elijah. "Abram, don't," I said. I'd already seen enough people die today. "Please, he's not worth it. Leave him there and come with us."

Abram didn't acknowledge my plea. He just kept walking. Past me. Past Mike. Past his own dead brother until he stood over Elijah's beaten body.

Elijah flinched. It was a subtle move, nothing more than a tiny twitch of the jaw and a hesitation in the way he pushed himself up off the ground. For the first time since we'd stumbled into Purity Springs, we posed a threat. His precious Eden had seen him for who he truly was. His only son, the future of his blessed prophecy, had turned on him. And Abram was glaring down at him with the full intent of gutting his own uncle.

Elijah's gaze swept from Joseph to me before settling on Eden. She was still standing at the edge of the fields, staring at the pool of blood circling James's body.

"Eden, go," he yelled, commanding her into motion. "Go back to the community center. Tell them of the evil these four have brought forth and bring your uncles back with you."

Eden hesitated, took a tiny step forward, then stopped,

horror and disbelief etched on her face. Whatever innocence she'd managed to maintain was gone, destroyed the second she'd seen her father's blood-soaked hands.

"Eden?" Joseph inched toward her, his hands held out as if he was begging her not to be frightened. "Come with us. You don't have to stay here."

Elijah smirked. "And who would take care of you on the outside, Eden? Who would keep you safe? Who would keep your actions in line with God's will?"

"I will. I will keep you safe, Eden."

The sincerity in Joseph's voice was so strong, so honest, that it tore my heart in two. I knew he was telling the truth. He'd walk through the fires of hell for his sister, and right now, he was going to risking his life for the chance to do it.

"Remember what you've been taught, Eden. Nothing but vanity, greed, and evil lurk beyond this town. They are proof if it," Elijah said, sweeping a hand in my direction.

Joseph paled. I couldn't help but wonder if he believed his father, if somehow, even for a fleeting moment, he held me responsible for his cousin's death.

"Don't lis—" I started to say, but Joseph cut me off.

"He's lying, Eden," Joseph said. "He killed our mother. He shunned Aunt Mary and barred her from ever seeing James and Abram. He killed a boy my age, a complete stranger who'd done nothing to hurt him or this town. His only sin, *their* only sin"—Joseph motioned toward Mike and me— "was running out of gas, and yet for that he killed one of them."

Eden didn't respond. Her attention was on Joseph, but her mind appeared to be a thousand miles away.

"You saw him kill James. His own nephew," Joseph continued. "For what, Eden? Because God told him to? Because he was trying to keep this town pure? No God is that evil, Eden. No God!"

"Joseph?" Her voice quivered as she took a tentative step forward.

Joseph sighed, his posture relaxing as he held her hand out to her. "Yes, Eden?"

"I love you," she said, and then she turned and ran.

THIRTY-SIX

Joseph dropped to his knees, the tears slipping from his eyes as he watched his sister run back toward town, back to a life that she'd never escape.

Elijah struggled to his feet, gagging on the mist of red he coughed up. The side of his lip was split and blood trailed from his nose, mingling with the smile etched on his face.

"Eden will bring them back," he crooned. "You will not escape judgment. You will perish because you refused, *refused*, to see the truth and be saved. What awaits you is not resurrection but damnation."

Joseph studied his father, not a hint of defeat in his posture, not a glint of anger in his eyes. I had no idea what he was thinking, no clue what he was preparing to do.

"You," he finally said. "You're no prophet. No saint. You're nothing."

Joseph stalked toward Elijah, his movements slow and steady. He looked at Abram clutching the blade and motioned for him to move. Abram hesitated, then shuffled slightly, his features twisted in confusion.

"You killed my mother. You killed James. You killed Dee's boyfriend. Eventually, you'll kill me too."

Elijah shook his head. "I didn't *kill* anyone, Joseph. I gave them a choice, and they chose wrong."

I could practically see Joseph's resolve solidifying. He'd spent months planning their escape, trying desperately to preserve Eden's innocence and his own sanity. Now he'd bathe in his own father's blood if that was what it took.

"Joseph, please. Don't do this," I begged. I felt the desire for revenge pulsing through my body too, craved that sliver of satisfaction I'd get from watching Elijah die a cold, hard death at my own hands. But if we stayed here any longer, we were screwed. I had no doubt Eden would bring the entire town back with her, and I wanted to be long gone when that happened. "Leave him and let's go."

"Your God's will is no match for mine!" Joseph yelled, ignoring my plea. He launched himself at his father, twisting Elijah's arm behind his back. "I watched you inflict pain on those who strayed. I memorized every sadistic punishment you used on me. And I must say, *Father*, you taught me well."

I winced as Joseph gave one last heave upward and a dull crack broke through the thick night air. Elijah screamed, his face contorting in a mixture of shock and pain.

Joseph released him and shoved him to the ground, hovering above his father as if trying to decide what to do next.

He made up his mind, and a calm determination settled over him. Elijah had taken his childhood, his mother, and his sister. Now Joseph was going to take his life.

I tried to drown out the sound of Joseph's attack. Elijah's grunts had become nothing but a steady stream of gurgling moans. Bone against body. Skin against skin. The punches came one after another. I stopped counting when I hit double digits and started humming to myself, trying to drown them all out.

"Stop." The word flew from my mouth and Mike swung his head in my direction, as stunned with my plea as me. But I couldn't do it, couldn't stand there and watch Joseph pummel his father into the ground. No matter how much I hated this town, no matter how much I wanted this twisted man to pay for Luke's death, I *would not* become him. And I sure as hell wouldn't let Joseph either.

"Joseph, please. Stop."

Eventually, I heard silence. Joseph's deathly promises died out, giving way to a terrifying calm. I swallowed hard as I looked at Elijah's body. His breaths were shallow, his chest rising in jerky movements. He was alive; barely, but he was alive.

"We gotta go," I choked out. It was only a matter of time before Eden came back with her uncles and Elijah's loyal following in tow. If we were lucky, if we left now, maybe we'd have a ten-minute head start.

Splatters of blood shone on Joseph's face, and his eyes were dark but not apologetic. He had years of emotional crap to sort through, and if anyone knew how painfully screwed up that road was going to be, it was me. But now wasn't the time.

"Can you walk?" I asked Mike. It was obvious he was in pain. He was shaking, and his jaw was clenched so tight I wondered how he could breathe.

"I'm fine, Dee. Just give me a minute," he ground out and slowly straightened up. "Go get him."

I followed Mike's line of site across the street and saw Abram sitting on the ground next to James's body, mumbling something incoherent. He looked broken, hollow to the point that I doubted he even knew where he was anymore. All I could hear was what sounded like a nursery rhyme traveling in the wind between us.

"Abram!" I said, hoping to jar him back to the present.

"Leave him," Joseph said. "We don't have time."

I knew what he meant. It would take time to get through to Abram, to convince him to leave his brother in the middle of the street and come with us. Precious minutes we didn't have.

THIRTY-SEVEN

The three of us kept to the edges of the fields, running parallel to the main road. I kept looking back, searching for headlights or torches or God knows whatever else those people might come after us with.

The lights from the town faded, but I kept running until my legs burned and my sides ached. Then I ran some more.

There was nothing in front of us but darkness. The moon was lost, the clouds closing in long before the cold. I fell to the ground, struggling to catch my breath as the first snowflakes began to fall. Neither Mike nor Joseph urged me to move, and I sat there, shaking. I'd been surviving on fear and terror alone. Given the space to breathe and the illusion of safety, everything came crashing down, a massive implosion focused solely on me.

My body shuddered with sobs so intense they lacked

sound. My chest was ripped in pain, tears searing paths down my frozen cheeks. Mike tried to comfort me, laying his cheek on the top of my head and whispering something soothing.

"I left him there," I choked out. I'd spent hours plotting and planning a way to get Luke out, agreeing to anything and everything. Then I'd left him there, cold and alone.

"We didn't have a choice, Dee," Joseph said.

I didn't agree. We'd had plenty of choices, but somehow we'd managed to make all the wrong ones.

Mike took my hand, clasping it tighter when I went to pull away. "You're going to listen to me, Dee, then you're going to get up and keep going." I nodded and let my hand relax into his. "Luke made me swear that no matter what happened to him, I'd get you out. He wouldn't want to slow us down, wouldn't want you to waste one second sitting here worrying about him."

"I know, but that doesn't—"

Mike put a finger to my lips, silencing me. "I can't do this alone, Dee. I need you to get up and walk. *Luke* needs you to get up and walk."

My shoulders heaved in time with my sobs. Mike was right. From the first time I told Luke about my past, broke down and shared with him the disgusting details that rotted me from the inside out, he'd understood. He'd promised me it was going to be okay, that somehow I'd be okay, that he would make sure of it. Every fiber of my being believed him back then; I still did now. Luke would protect me no matter what it cost him. But I'd never expected it to be his life.

What seemed like an eternity ticked by as we struggled

through the cold night. We passed our first town about five hours out. Its twinkling lights flickered in the distance, causing a familiar sense of unease to sweep over me. What were the names of the towns Elijah's brothers controlled? Had Joseph ever told me?

Paranoia settled into my body like a dull ache, and I made my way farther away from the road. I wasn't getting near those lights. I'd trust nobody but the two boys standing next to me. That was my new creed ... at least until I got home, till I heard Mrs. Hooper's gentle voice promising me everything would be okay.

"What are the names of those towns your uncles work in?" I asked.

"You want to head in, see if they have a phone or a police department or something?" Mike asked before Joseph had a chance to answer.

"No," I replied quickly. "We don't know anything about that town ... about the people."

Mike didn't fully know what we were up against. He hadn't been at the chapel; he hadn't seen Elijah's brothers.

Joseph flashed me a dark look, confirming my fears. We were too close. "I think we need to get as far out as possible. At least to the next county if we can. Then we need to find you some help," he said.

We made it two more hours before Mike waved us to a stop and sank to the ground. His breathing was labored, and a fine sheen of sweat covered his face. The strip of fabric we'd tied around his shoulder had turned completely red; I carefully peeled it away, praying for the best while expecting the worst. Blood trickled out, the wound swollen and angry. I prodded at the unbroken skin. It was warm, hot, despite the bits of snow landing on it.

Mike grabbed my hand and growled, "Stop poking at it, Dee. It's hurts."

"I know, but—"

"But nothing. Leave it alone."

Joseph tore a strip of fabric from the hem of his shirt and pushed me out of the way. "Let me re-tie it. You've got to keep pressure on it or you'll lose too much blood."

"Don't touch me." Mike's words were laced with so much hatred that I cringed. I felt bad for Joseph. He was trying, but no matter what he did, he'd never be able to redeem himself. Not to Mike anyway.

Joseph quickly recovered himself and turned toward me, calm and completely in control. I shuddered as I watched his entire tone shift, like one mask was being traded for another. Thoughts of Elijah floated to the surface and I quickly pushed them away. I didn't have the time or the strength to consider their similarities, never mind acknowledge that Elijah's blood ran through Joseph's veins.

He handed me the piece of fabric he'd torn from his shirt, motioning me toward Mike. "Wrap it around his shoulder and tie it off tight so he doesn't continue to bleed."

I looked at Mike for permission. "Fine, but make it quick. We got to keep moving," he said.

I folded the make-shift bandage in half and gently laid it against Mike's shoulder. He swore and jerked back. Gritting my teeth, I pressed my hand against the wound, ignoring his sharp inhale of breath and pained expression.

Blood quickly seeped through the bandage, coating my fingers as I applied pressure. I wished Mike had let his guard down long enough for Joseph to handle this.

Joseph carefully doled out directions, and I couldn't help but wonder how often he had done this exact same thing. How many times had he patched someone up, or stopped someone's bleeding? I wondered if he'd done it to his mother, to himself.

Mike's pace was painfully slow for the remainder of the walk. His color was fading, his words becoming nearly inaudible. He stopped suddenly and hunched over, retching up nothing but stomach bile. It was that smear of red mingled with his spit that changed my mind, had me willing to venture out onto the road and flag down the next car that passed by.

"I can't do this anymore," Mike said as he swiped an arm across his mouth.

He lowered himself to the ground and propped himself up against a tree stump. His eyes momentarily fluttered shut, and I panicked. Reaching down, I grabbed his shoulder and shook him hard.

"Mike? What do you mean you can't do this anymore? You have no choice."

"That hurts," he mumbled, sliding away from me. His tears were clear, carving their way through the dirt and blood on his face. "Go, Dee. Leave me here and go."

"No." I tucked my shoulder under his arm and tried to

get him to stand. As long as we were moving, no matter how slowly, we had a chance.

"You don't get it, Dee. I've got nothing to go back to. Luke is dead. He's dead."

I wound my fingers into Mike's and squeezed. Like him, I knew what getting back meant for both of us. Everything at school, at home, even the stupid candy bar wrappers on the floor of my car would remind us of Luke.

"That's not true," I said, reaching for something, any promise of a future that would get him to keep going. "You have me."

"Get up," Joseph said to me, and I did, then waited to see what he planned to do. He bent down next to Mike and stared at him, silently demanding him to move.

"No. Leave me. I'm dead weight anyway. Besides, I promised Luke I'd keep her safe." Mike paused and choked back a sob. "You want to help, you want to be forgiven, then leave me here and make sure she gets home."

"And you think that will absolve me? Watching you stay behind and die?"

Mike went to respond, to answer Joseph's rage with a bit of his own, but Joseph waved him off. "I don't want to hear it. You promised your brother you'd get her home. *You!* And that's exactly what you're going to do. Now get up."

Recognition flashed violently across Mike's face, and I held out my hand, willing what little strength I had left into him. "Please," I begged. "We're so close. So close."

Joseph half-carried Mike the rest of the way, his arm tucked under Mike's shoulder's so he could bear most of his weight. Dawn broke, and only then did the chill wrapping around me begin to fade and exhaustion take over. I struggled to remember the days, the hours, I'd spent trapped in Elijah's hold. They were melding together into one big blur.

"What day is it?" I asked as I slowed to a crawl.

"Sunday," Joseph replied. "Why?"

I shrugged. The information was of absolutely no importance, but the knowledge was soothing nonetheless.

"Look," Mike said a moment later, his finger pointing to the road sign ahead.

I squinted, then took a dangerous few steps into the open and read it. *Henley.*

I recognized that name. I didn't know a soul in that town, but I definitely recognized the name. Luke and Mike had played there less than a month ago. I'd driven the whole two hours to watch them get their asses kicked, only to be told that they couldn't ride home with me. Apparently school policy dictated they take the team bus to and from *all* games.

Henley was a far cry from the safety of home, but it was a start. This was our best chance of getting Mike somewhere safe, somewhere where absolutely no one related to Elijah Hawkins could touch us.

It was early. The walkways were littered with morning's papers, the streets quiet. A dog barked, its owner swearing at it for making too much noise. That sound alone, that foul four-letter word shattering the morning silence, let me know that we had re-entered the land of the sane.

But I wasn't going to ask the dog's owner for help or

knock on any doors. I was going to keep walking, keep dragging Mike and Joseph with me until I found the only familiar place in this town—the high school.

I climbed the wide steps to the front doors of the school. I'd walked through them three weeks ago in search of a bathroom. The school was active then, kids roaming the halls while the janitor worked around them, sweeping the floors.

Since it was Sunday, the school was locked up tight, but I yanked on the doors anyway before settling down on the front steps. My frozen body sank into the concrete, and for the first time in what seemed like an eternity, I closed my eyes and let my mind go. I had every intention of staying right there until somebody found us.

THIRTY-EIGHT

They said I slept for two days straight, woke up screaming Elijah's name. It was Mrs. Hooper's soothing voice and the familiar scent of her lavender hand cream that finally allowed my mind to clear, drove home the recognition that I was safe.

Even then, I didn't fight the drugs the doctors gave me. Sleep offered me an out, a safe, unconscious place where Luke was still alive, sitting beside me.

"Hey there, Dee."

The familiar voice echoed through my dreams. I swore for a second it was Luke, that the strong hand stroking mine was his. I opened my eyes, a smile already forming on my lips when his face came into focus.

"Mike?" I asked.

"It's me," he said, moving from the chair to the bed. His right arm was in a sling and there were stitches across his cheek.

He looked tired and beaten down, and his hair was messed up. I reached up to smooth it and he caught my hand, squeezing it gently before lowering it back to the bed.

I glanced up at the clock hanging above the door. It was three a.m. "Are you okay?" I asked, curious as to why he was sitting here next to me and not asleep in his own room.

He tried for a smile, but his entire expression was shadowed in grief. "We made it to Henley. You're safe now."

"Did you tell them about Luke?" I asked. I didn't remember anyone trying to question me. I didn't know how much the doctors knew, or what part, if any, of the truth Mike had told them.

Mike grabbed my hand and brought it to his cheek, then turned his head so I couldn't see his pain. But I felt it, felt the steady stream of his tears covering my palm. "I'm sorry, Dee."

Sorry? What did he have to be sorry about? "Did you tell them? Did you tell them what happened to Luke? Did you tell them about Elijah and James?"

"I did," he said, turning back to me. "But they don't believe me. Nobody does."

"What? Why?"

"I told the police everything—about us running out of gas, about the irrigation shed and James. I told them everything, Dee. *Everything*. But they think we made it up, that we're suffering from some sort of post-traumatic stress thing."

That didn't make any sense. The images in my mind were real. The feel of Luke's dead body, his cold hands, James's blood covering my feet... those images were too vivid, too real for me to have imagined them.

I frantically kicked the blanket away and struggled to sit up. My arms were bandaged from wrist to elbow and I tore at the gauze, frustrated by its strength. When I had the last bit of it unraveled, I thrust my arms in Mike's direction. They were cut up—seven nearly identical slices marring my skin, eight if you counted Elijah's binding mark on my palm.

"What about these? How do you explain these?"

"They think you tried to kill yourself. That after the accident, after Luke … well, they think you did that to yourself."

"What accident?" I yelled. "What the hell are you talking about? There was no accident."

"My dad and Mr. Hooper went to Purity Springs. They spent two days there with the police, asking questions and talking to Elijah. All they found was our mangled car lodged against a tractor. The officer they talked to in Purity Springs claimed it was a car accident, that the puncture in my shoulder and Luke's injuries are consistent with the accident."

Mike's eyes met mine, and for a moment I could feel his tension, knew that the words he was about to utter were going to be bad. "According to the official report, I went through the windshield. That's why I'm cut up."

"But what about Luke?" I cried, remembering his body lying there on the ground, the blood from James's throat edging closer to his tattered jeans. "What about James? What did they say about them?"

"They never found James. There's no record of him or his brother at all. It's as if they never existed."

I stared at Mike, stunned. Joseph had told me his father

was capable of fabricating entire lives. I'd watched him do it to me. But to deny the existence of his own nephews…

"Luke? What did they say about him?" I asked again.

Mike sighed and ran a hand through his hair, a mindless habit that made my entire body ache for Luke. "We buried him yesterday. The medical examiner from Purity Springs did an autopsy. They cremated his body, told my parents it'd be best if they didn't see him first."

"Why the hell not?" I yelled. Why wouldn't Luke's parents want to see him—dead or alive—one last time?

"The report says he was thrown from the car, that he got caught up in the chisel plow we hit. He was mangled beyond recognition."

I knew what a chisel plow was, the rusted eight-inch shanks meant to loosen the soil. And there hadn't been a chisel plow anywhere near our car, never mind a tractor. "That's a lie," I screamed.

I got out of the bed, began the frantic search for my clothes. I wanted my shoes. I wanted a pair of jeans. I wanted to walk out of this place and back to Purity Springs so I could haul Elijah Hawkins back here and make him tell the truth.

I found my muddy clogs in the room's lone closet. Shoved in the left one was the doll Eden had given me. I took it out and brought it to my nose, inhaled the rotted scent. I tossed it to the ground; I'd drag Eden here as well if that's what it took.

I shoved my feet into the clogs and went about untying my hospital gown. The sooner I was dressed, the sooner I could prove that my nightmare was true.

"They sent their apologies, you know."

"Who?" I asked, scanning the hallway. The only person I could see out there was the night nurse, and she was staring at her phone, laughing as she texted away.

"Elijah. The town," Mike answered.

"Did you tell him to go screw himself?"

"It's not that easy," he replied. I tossed my hands out, motioning for him to explain. "They managed to come up with this whole bullshit story, claimed we left Luke and wandered off in search of help. Elijah said that if he'd known there was more than one person in the car, he would've sent out a search party to find us, made sure we got medical care sooner."

I had no doubt Elijah had sent out a search party, one armed with knives and Bibles.

"That doesn't make any sense. I mean, we know names and details. We wouldn't know all that... *couldn't* know that if we hadn't been there. They can't explain away everything that happened."

"He can and he did. According to city records, there's no Elijah Hawkins. The mayor of that town is a man named John Smith. He had a wife named Abigail, but she died a few weeks ago of cancer."

"What about Joseph and Eden? Are there any records of them?"

"Fourteen-year-old daughter, Evelyn. No son listed, or so my dad says."

I shook my head, trying hard to understand what Mike was saying. "What about Joseph? I mean, he was with us. Surely he could back up our story. Get him. Tell him—"

"He's gone, Dee."

I frantically grasped at my last memories before waking up in the hospital. Henley. The high school and the enormous blue door I used as a pillow. Joseph sitting there next to me, tucking me into his side as I gave in to exhaustion. He was there. Joseph was there. "What do you mean, he's gone?"

"I fell asleep right after you and woke up to the school's principal nudging my foot. No one was there with us. No one."

I brought my hands to my head and squeezed. Digging my fingers into my scalp, I tried uselessly to claw Mike's words from my mind. Joseph was gone. I'd done everything I could to help him. Bled for him. Bound myself to his father. Risked Mike's life and gotten Luke killed. All for him. All so that he could have the *chance* to save his sister, and this was how he thanked me. *This!*

The sound that ripped from my throat was feral, a cross between a sob and a war cry. I wasn't crazy, and no doctor or police report could convince me I was.

"Do you believe it happened? Tell me you remember it. Luke. The house. The basement … all of it."

"They think I'm crazy, Dee, that I feel guilty I lived and Luke didn't. I needed to talk to you before they did, to see if you remember it the same way, prove to myself that I'm not going insane."

Mike picked up my hand and ran his fingers across the thin pink ribbon of scars. "I spent two days waiting for you to wake up, Dee. Two days listening to the doctors' explanations and swallowing their pills, but it didn't stop. The memories, the sounds, the smells, everything that happened in Purity Springs is stuck in my mind, but I couldn't get out of that room, that ward, until I said what they wanted to hear."

"What are you saying?"

"I'm saying that when my dad comes in here this morning, when the cops or Mrs. Hooper ask you what happened, you lie. Tell them it was an accident, that we hit a plow and left Luke there to go find help."

Something in my mind shifted, a horrifying realization suddenly making its way into my consciousness. "You said you told the cops everything. The cops—were they from Purity Springs?"

"Hell no. I wouldn't have let those bastards anywhere near me," he said. "There were two of them, a sheriff and one of his deputies. They were from some neighboring town. I don't remember the name. Elijah or John or whatever his name is apparently called them when I started talking. He thought it would be wise to have an 'uninvolved' third party do their own investigation."

Dropping my head, I dug my hands into the wounds on my arms to make sure I wasn't trapped in some hideous nightmare. The sharp burn told me I wasn't, and I glanced up and scanned the doorway to make sure no one was listening.

"Dee? Talk to me. What's going on?"

"His brother," I choked out. "Elijah has two brothers. They control the neighboring towns. One is a sheriff. The other sits on some sort of town council. That's how they fly under the radar. That's why none of the neighboring towns suspect a damn thing about Purity Springs. If *they* know..."

I trailed off, unwilling to vocalize my suspicions. If the officer who got Mike locked up in the psych ward was who I thought he was, then Elijah's brother had been here. Jared knew where we lived and how to find us.

THIRTY-NINE

I sat in the dark alone, the muted beeping of the machines keeping me tethered to my surroundings. Luke was dead. Joseph was gone. And Mike wanted me to lie, to pretend that none this had ever happened.

Mrs. Hooper opened my door and smiled. She looked exhausted and thin, as if she hadn't slept or eaten for days. She probably hadn't. I couldn't help but feel a bit of happiness. She'd worried about me. Cared about me. Missed me, and somehow that made everything a little brighter.

"It's nice to see you awake," she said as she hurried to my side. She looked me up and down, her gaze lingering on the clogs on my feet. "You're not going anywhere, young lady. You're going to get back in the bed and do exactly as the doctor says."

I waved her off. "I need my clothes. I want to go home. I want to see Luke."

She stopped at my words, her smile fading. "Luke is gone, sweetie. He died in the accident."

"I know he's gone," I said. "But it's not what you think. It didn't happen the way everybody is saying."

"What do you mean?"

There was a gentle assurance in her voice, the unspoken promise that she would listen and, at the very least, try to believe me.

I went to answer her, to tell her every sordid detail of my nightmare, when a knock on the door stopped me.

"It's Dee, right?" His voice was gentle and laced with false sympathy. "I'm Officer Smith, but you can call me Jared."

He was back in uniform, the gun and the shiny badge in clear view. He took a step closer and pulled off his hat, dipping his head politely toward Mrs. Hooper.

"If you're up to it, I'd like to ask you a few questions. I talked to your friend... ah..." Jared paused and scratched his head, then dug out a little notebook. He flipped through the pages until he found the name he was looking for.

I wasn't buying it. He knew Mike's name, probably knew his damn shoe size.

"Mike. I talked to your friend Mike, but I would like to hear what you have to say."

Under the stupid assumption that any of us had a choice, Mrs. Hooper motioned to the chair beside my bed. "If you can make it quick, please. She's tired and needs her rest."

"Absolutely, ma'am," he said. "But if you don't mind, I have to ask you to wait outside."

Confusion flickered across Mrs. Hooper's face. "She's a minor. Surely I'm able to stay in here with her?" She slid closer to me.

"Usually that's the case, but seeing as Dee is almost eighteen and technically a ward of the state, you'll need to wait outside."

I sank farther beneath the blankets and shot Mrs. Hooper a look, one I hoped she'd realize meant *under no circumstances can you leave me alone with this man.*

It didn't work. She just patted my shoulder and gave me a reassuring wink. "Ward of the state or not, she's like a daughter to me."

"I won't be more than ten minutes, ma'am," Jared promised. "I simply need to clarify some statements that Mike made, and then I'll be on my way. And you needn't worry. I'll treat her as if she were one of my own."

Mrs. Hooper nodded. "Thank you. I'm sure you will."

Jared closed the door and clicked the lock into place, then stood there staring at me. I glanced at the bathroom, then at the double window before inspecting the ceiling for cameras that might connect to the nurse's station. There was no way for me to get away.

He caught my fear and tipped his head to the side. "I understand your apprehension, but I have no intention of harming you."

That statement should have made me feel better. It

didn't, because left unsaid was the *not yet*. "Then why are you here?" I asked. "What do you want?"

"I want nothing from you. I merely wanted to express my condolences over the loss of your boyfriend." He leaned over my bed and rested his hands on either side of my pillow, caging me in. "It was an accident, exactly like Mike reported. But remember, accidents happen all the time, and at the most inopportune moments."

The first tear escaped, and he reached forward to brush it away. I pulled back, never wanting anybody to touch me again.

"No one needs to get hurt, Dee. No one," he murmured, easing himself away from my bed.

"Officer Smith," I said as he reached the door.

"Please, call me Jared."

I had to swallow twice in order to get my lips to form his name. "*Jared*. Where is Joseph?"

He sighed, as if answering my question, or rather not answering it, was too painful for him to bear. "Forget about Joseph, Dee. Forget about Elijah and Purity Springs and try to live your life."

I wanted to do as he suggested. I wanted to forget about what happened to Joseph and Eden...even Abram. I didn't want to care anymore; it hurt too much. Maybe Elijah's brother was right. Maybe the only way for me to survive was to forget.

EPILOGUE

Mrs. Hooper, Luke's parents, the school counselor ... everybody thinks I need to talk to someone, work through the long spells of silence that consume me. So every Tuesday at 4:15 I sit in a shrink's office, reciting the appropriate answers to his questions: *Yes, I'm doing okay in school. Yes, I've come to terms with losing Luke. Yes, I'm going to start becoming more involved with friends and school.*

His name is Carl, and he isn't that bad. At least he doesn't look at me like I'm crazy. But that's probably because I've done exactly as Mike instructed ... I've lied.

Outside of talking to Mike, I never utter Elijah Hawkins's name. It's better this way, keeps me protected and out of Elijah's reach. And out of his brothers' reach. It's not hard during the day, when I have school and Mike to distract me. But at night, when I wake up screaming and searching for Luke ... well, that's when my resolve falters.

Mrs. Hooper comes running into my room each time, begging me to talk to her. I've tried a few times, but the warning Jared delivered to me always stops me cold.

According to the doctors, the few memories we divulged while in the hospital were nothing more than delusions. Hallucinations brought on by severe concussions and trauma, or, in Mike's case, the inability to deal with Luke's death. They can all believe whatever they want; Mike and I know the truth.

I finally broke down and told Mike about my nightmares last week. He bought me a journal and told me to write my memories in there. I think he's afraid I'm going to slip up and say something to my shrink or to Mrs. Hooper. I get that; sometimes I'm afraid I will too.

The journal is hidden beneath my mattress. Each night, when the nightmares overtake my dreams, I reach for it and furiously scribble down every detail I can remember. I never re-read my entries, just fill up page after page like my own diary of proof. Proof that no one but me will ever see.

The same people who insisted I see a shrink keep promising me that things will get better, get easier with time. I can pretend all I want, but no amount of time or distance, not even a gravestone bearing Luke's name, can bring me peace. The only truth I know is that eventually the evil and darkness I struggled to escape will find its way back into my life... back into my soul.

Acknowledgments

Trisha Leaver

This book would not exist if it weren't for the support and encouragement of countless people. My agent, Kevan Lyon, whose unwavering belief in me as an author makes everything possible. My editor, Brian Farrey-Latz, and the entire Flux crew. My amazing CPs, who read countless version of *Creed* and never once questioned my sanity. And my co-author, Lindsay Currie, for taking this journey with me.

To my family...you will never know how much your love and support means to me. Meme, who every summer would let me stay up to the wee hours of the morning reading her Stephen King collection. Kyle and his band of friends. Your antics are a constant source of inspiration for my male characters. My sweet Caroline, whose refusal to subscribe to the word "impossible" guides my every move. Casey, whose gentle soul and huge smile reminds me never to take life to too seriously. And my husband, Brian, the keeper of my secrets and the love of my life. Your patience and strength are what keeps me whole.

Lindsay Currie

I'd like to thank *so many* people it's ridiculous, but I realize it isn't possible to mention everyone who made this dream a reality by name. With that in mind, I'm going to rein myself in and keep this simple. A *huge* thank you goes out to the following people, because without them, *Creed* would not exist:

My husband John. You're the creamer to my coffee, babe. Thanks for everything, especially that sense of humor of yours that kept me smiling…even through the rejections.

My son Rob. What can I say, except that you're amazing? You've become a determined and kind tennis player who shows so much heart on the court that I'm proud to say you are a huge inspiration to me.

My son Ben. You're a champion both in your sport and in my heart. You've become a sensitive and strong martial artist whose behavior on and off the mat has taught me what it means to truly give 100 percent.

My daughter Ella. My Little Mama and princess with a heart of gold. You've become a true advocate for manatees who reminds me every single day that anything is possible.

I'd also like to thank my parents for encouraging me every single day as a child to follow my dreams, and for reminding me that anything is possible if you put your mind to it.

A huge thanks goes out to everyone who read *Creed* in its early stages (you know who you are!). We couldn't have done this without you.

Thank you also to my agent, Kathleen Rushall, for the miracles she works and to Brian Farrey-Latz and the whole team at Flux for taking a chance on *Creed*—the little book that could.

Last but not least, thank you to Trisha Leaver, my co-author, for writing this with me. I've enjoyed every single moment of it.

© Boule Photography

Trisha Leaver graduated from the University of Vermont with a degree in Social Work. She is a member of SCBWI, the Horror Writers Association, and the Cape Cod Children's Writers. Visit her online at www.trishaleaver.com.

© Alan Klehr

Lindsay Currie graduated from Knox College and is a member of SCBWI, the Horror Writers Association, the YA Scream Queens, and OneFourKidLit, a community of authors with debuts in 2014. Visit her online at www.lindsaycurrie.com.